RANDOM

In Case I Don't Make It

By Earl Snort

TotalRecall Publications, Inc.
1103 Middlecreek
Friendswood, Texas 77546
281-992-3131 Tel
www.totalrecallpress.com

All rights reserved. Except as permitted under the United States Copyright Act of 1976, No part of this publication may be reproduced, stored in a retrieval system, or transmitted in any form or by any means electronic or mechanical or by photocopying, recording, or otherwise without prior permission of the publisher. Exclusive worldwide content publication / distribution by TotalRecall Publications, Inc.

Copyright © 2025 by Earl Snort
Illustrations by Susan C. Barnes via AI

ISBN: 978-1-64883-2789
UPC: 6-43977-42789-2

Library of Congress Control Number: 2025931734

FIRST EDITION

1 2 3 4 5 6 7 8 9 10

This is a work of fiction. The characters, names, events, views, and subject matter of this book are either the author's imagination or are used fictitiously. Any similarity or resemblance to any real people, real situations or actual events is purely coincidental and not intended to portray any person, place, or event in a false, disparaging or negative light.

The scanning, uploading and distribution of this book via the Internet or via any other means without the permission of the publisher is illegal and punishable by law. Please purchase only authorized electronic editions, and do not participate in or encourage electronic piracy of copyrighted materials. Your support of the author's rights is appreciated.

It's all a pack of lies. Not a speck of it is true.
Earl Snort, 2025

DEDICATION

As always, this book is dedicated to my wife of 53 years. It's also dedicated to our brave law enforcement officers and military servicemen.

Many thanks to JFW, a military compadre for 56 years, for proofing the draft of this book and making corrections. Any mistakes are mine alone.

"Hello darkness, my old friend. I've come to talk to you again. Because a vision softly creeping left its seeds while I was sleeping, and the vision that was planted in my brain still remains in the sound of silence . . . ."

The Sound of Silence - Simon & Garfunkel - 1964 - (Better Performance by Disturbed - 2015)

"I'll wait in this room where the sun never shines. Wait in this place where the shadows run from themselves."

White Room - Cream - 1968

"Good morning, America. How are you? So don't you know me? I'm your native son . . . ."

City of New Orleans - Arlo Guthrie - 1972

"Welcome to your life. There's no turning back . . . . Help me make the most of freedom . . . . Nothing lasts forever. Everybody wants to rule the world."

Everybody Wants to Rule the World - Tears for Fears - 1985

"Yeah, it's okay. It's so nice. Just another day in paradise. Well there's no place I'd rather be. Well, it's two hearts and one dream. I wouldn't trade it for anything, and I ask the Lord every night, ooh for just another day in paradise."

Just Another Day in Paradise - Phil Collins - 1989

-Prologue-
The Dilemma

My name is Chester A. (for Arnold) Sinclair. I was born on Leap Day in 1904, in the City of Louisville, Jefferson County, Commonwealth of Kentucky, United States of America. I still reside there 69 years later as a taxpaying, voting citizen. I thought I was done with drama, but I was wrong. Someone is trying to kill me and I don't know who it is. I don't know why.

So far as I know, I haven't had an enemy in years, perhaps even decades. I don't have enough information to report this to the cops, and I should know. I served as a Louisville city police officer for 38 years. I know how cops think and how they operate. They're not going to waste their time chasing shadows and I don't blame them. Right now shadows are all I've got. Forewarned is forearmed and so I am.

Besides, I don't have much in the way of theft-worthy assets, but I will protect what is mine. I haven't been robbed or burgled. I haven't even been threatened, but nevertheless, parties unknown have tried to kill me twice in the past three weeks. Whatever it is, it doesn't appear to be about money. It's got to be something personal.

I'm not screwing anyone's wife, nor have I stolen anything, nor even had a bitter argument with anyone in years. That's why this is so baffling. I once was a warrior, but I was never a T-Rex. I don't believe in a scorched Earth policy. I know my limitations - legally, physically, and emotionally. My cause has always been in defense of Mom, the American flag, and apple pie. I'm for America.

That's it. I'm a good guy - not a villain.

So . . . . I'm taking time now to put these random thoughts and our family history down on paper for posterity should I die, either by natural causes or at the hand of unknown assailant(s). Besides, I'm closer to the End than the Beginning. I want my daughter to know her heritage, which like many others her age, she's hardly ever pondered. Life's been good for her in middle-class America, like it's been for me and my Scottish-born parents. Arabella needs to pay attention and be vigilant. "Life, liberty, and the pursuit of happiness" are only one generation away from extinction if we don't keep the predators at bay, be they foreign or domestic. Once you lose it, it's gone forever. It would be a crying shame if we lost it after our forefathers fought and died 200 years ago to make it so, and likewise, each succeeding generation which followed suit to keep it.

-1-
Background

My parents, Angus R. (Randolph) Sinclair and Colleen Eliza Sinclair née Brodie, emigrated from Edinburgh, Scotland in 1892. My father was 22 years old and my mother was 18. In America, the 1890s were known as "The Gay 90s" because prosperity abounded. It wasn't so gay in Scotland when they departed. Times were hard there. I know very little about my grandparents, except to say my paternal grandfather, Elijah Sinclair, was a cobbler.

I'm not exactly sure why my parents settled in Louisville, but I think Papa had a sponsor. Maybe it was someone where he worked. There were a number of native-born Scots employed there. If Papa ever said, I wasn't paying attention. Whatever the reason, it's lost to posterity now.

My folks leased a small house at 718 South Floyd Street, and we lived there from the beginning of time in 1892, Anno Domini. Papa got a job right away at the Louisville & Nashville Railroad (L&N), starting on the bottom rung as a brakeman. Mama and Papa were always true blue to L&N. A dozen years later Papa became an engineer and our standard of living greatly improved. Suffice it to say, my parents were Scottish and they knew how to squeeze a nickel until the buffalo excreted. [See Indian Head/Buffalo Nickel circa 1913-1938.]

Angus, Jr. was born in 1898. He was followed by Phoebe in 1900, Claude in 1901, Theodore in 1903, and then me in 1904. I was the baby of the family.

Papa was proud as a banty rooster to become an American citizen. Mama, too. Both of them loved this country passionately. We always had an American flag hanging from a pole on our front porch. The first one only had 46 stars. Then New Mexico became a state and we got a new one with 47. A few months later, Arizona became a state and we bought an even newer one with 48, and it remained that way until some years after both Papa and Mama passed away.

The Spanish blew up the battleship USS Maine in February of 1898. At least that's what the newspapers reported. Neither my siblings nor I were even a gleam in Papa's eye when it happened, so none of us could say with authority. Nevertheless, in June, the Commonwealth of Kentucky along with every other state and territory, began recruiting volunteers from each of the various militias to go fight the nefarious Iberian hordes down in the Caribbean, and later in the Pacific. It was no surprise to anyone in Papa's hemisphere that he wanted to go. My mother didn't even try to dissuade him. His mind was made up.

Papa rode the L&N for free to Lexington, and enlisted in Company H, 1st Kentucky Volunteer Infantry Regiment. His unit arrived in Puerto Rico two days before the Spanish surrendered. He never fired a shot in anger, but it wasn't because he was unwilling. The conflict in the Caribbean had ended, but the 1st remained there as part of the occupation forces until they were mustered out in Louisville in February of 1899. They received a hero's welcome. The next day, Papa returned to work back at his old job at L&N. He said he even got a raise as a reward for his service to country.

Several years later, after most of the American population had forgotten all about the Spanish War, the veterans from Company H, as well as many other companies, were awarded the Spanish War Campaign Service Medal. The ribbon was a burnt amber with two wide, dark blue vertical stripes. The medal itself was a bronze disk. It had a Spanish blockhouse on the obverse with the inscription, *War With Spain*, and *1898*. The reverse had an American eagle with the inscription, *United States Army For Service*. Papa wore that medal on the lapel of his dress coat until the day he died. Mama passed it down to Angus, Jr., being he was born before Papa returned from the war.

We grew up in a serious God-fearing, thrifty, hardworking household. My siblings and I all graduated from high school. No slackers in the Sinclair household! The topic regarding the necessity for education never once came up for discussion. It was implicitly understood by all. Our parents had been intermittently and poorly educated. Education was the key to success. It was do or die. No excuses. All us boys went to Male High School. Phoebe went to Female High School. Back then, they were the only public high schools in Louisville.

My passion has always been baseball. None of my brothers were allowed to play school sports. No time for frivolous pursuits. They were expected to get back home after school as soon as possible to carry out whatever part-time jobs they had. However, by the time I was a junior, Papa relented. I tried out and made the team both my junior and senior years. I rode the plank most of my junior year; however, I was the starting right fielder as a senior. I played every single game, batting .306 with two home runs. Believe it or not, back then those were barely above average statistics. We put up 9 wins against 6 losses for the season. Afterwards, I was awarded an amber, pullover letterman's sweater with a violet, felt-backed, chenille H (for High School) centered in the chest. The letter had an embossed gold emblem of a baseball centered above crossed bats. The letter meant as much to me as my father's medal meant to him. I still have it, but now it fits a mite too snug for comfort.

I graduated in 1922, smack-dab in the middle of my class academically. I was neither an owl nor a goat. Now it was time for me to earn my own living. I wasn't getting kicked out of the nest yet, being the only child still living at home. That would have broken Mama's heart, but I needed to find a full-time job to maintain family values. You know, as a God-fearing, patriotic, hardworking, American citizen. It was same-old, same-old for all of us, regarding membership and regular attendance at the Presbyterian Church of the United States over on 4th Street. Like I mentioned before, there are no slackers in the Sinclair family. Nothing had changed just because I graduated. In fact, expectations had increased for me. To wit:

Angus, Jr. had followed Papa to the railroad. He was doing well. He married a gal named Carla Stokes. They had a baby boy appropriately named Angus III. They called him Trey for short.

Phoebe married a baker named Hiram Cornaby. He worked in the family bakery with his father and brother. They had a bonnie lass named Anastasia and a wee boy named Ernest.

Claude joined the United States Navy. Nobody expected it, but he stayed for 30 years. He never married. He only came home on leave once, right after his basic training, but he did send postcards from exotic ports around the world. One time he sent Mama a silk scarf from China. A photograph of him in a white uniform as a 3rd class petty officer, while he was on liberty in the Philippines, hung proudly in our parlor. I never mentioned that it looked like he was standing in front of a brothel if you looked closely enough. He had a big grin on his face. Mama just thought he was happy, and I bet he was.

Theodore got on at the Ford assembly plant at 3rd Street and Eastern Parkway near Belknap Campus, new home to the University of Louisville. He was engaged to a lass named Abigail Dabney. Her father worked at the *Louisville Courier-Journal* newspaper as a typesetter.

That was the Sinclair Family Hall of Fame in May of 1922. Then there was me.

I didn't have a love interest at the time. In June, I went to work for the City of Louisville as a messenger, running back and forth from City Hall, sometimes riding a bike to the various departments throughout the city. It didn't pay a lot, but I got to know the all the department heads and the movers and shakers in and around both the City of Louisville and Jefferson County governments. (The City government was by far more prominent with more tax money than Jefferson County back then.) My working acquaintances included Louisville Mayor John H. Buschemeyer and Jefferson County

Judge W.H. Davidson, a position which besides being the county's lone circuit court judge, was also the county executive over the three elected county supervisors. I'm not saying either potentate ever invited me to eat dinner with them. Au contraire. All I mean is that I met them, and they recognized me and knew my name when they saw me.

Papa was a little perplexed by my choice of occupation. He believed wholeheartedly in Government in the abstract, but he was dubious of the politicians. He told me many a time to watch myself because politicians have a tendency to be shady. They seldom live up to their promises, and they tend to have slick and evasive answers when questioned about it. Nevertheless, he thought it was a good idea to have a son working inside the local government. He said I would have an opportunity to see how the politicians act in private. It would help us decide who to vote for. I had his whole-hearted blessing, and that was important to me.

Also in June, in a fevered rush of patriotism and wanting to follow in Papa's footsteps, I enlisted in Company C, 1st Infantry Regiment, Kentucky Militia. Of course, being a minor, it required Papa's signed permission. Back in those days, the militia was financed solely by the Commonwealth of Kentucky. No militia was affiliated whatsoever with the U.S. Army, except during time of war. Even so, all states and territories had a militia.

In 1924 by an Act of Congress and with the stroke of a pen, all state militias became federally recognized and put under the auspices of the newly formed National Guard Bureau in Washington, D.C. Each militia still belonged to the Governor of its respective state, but the President could take control over them whenever he saw fit. The federalization was done primarily to standardize training, and to bring the militias closer to the Regular Army in terms of military competencies whenever they were augmented into active duty. Also, it meant Uncle Sam ponied up much of the cost, not an insignificant matter to a poor state or commonwealth such as Mississippi or Louisiana, or Kentucky.

In Company C, we drilled at the Louisville Armory one evening a week, usually on a Tuesday. We attended a two-week bivouac each summer in what remained of Camp Zachary Taylor from the Great War. (Zachary Taylor had been an Army General, U.S. President, and a native son to Kentucky.) The camp was way out in the county off Poplar Level Road where one could shoot a gun in any direction and not hit a living soul, at least not one a city slicker was much concerned about. The city trolley didn't go all the way out there, so I had to walk another mile each way to report for duty.

Different from the Regular Army, there was no standardized basic training for the militia. That doesn't mean we didn't train. We most certainly did. We did calisthenics, and ran, and performed close order drill. We marched and studied and practiced small unit infantry tactics. We practiced hand-to-hand combat and riot control. We also trained extensively with the rifle and bayonet each summer, every single day for two weeks. It was the only time we shot each year, so it was really important. I'm proud to report that I became quite a good marksman. In fact, had I been Regular Army, I would have been awarded an Expert Rifleman's Badge. I had the distinction of that achievement within the militia itself, but without the emolument in the form of an Army Expert Rifleman's Badge.

One other little tidbit. Fighting with a bayonet was not my idea of a good time. Just the opposite. In my humble opinion, if it ever came down to that, someone in charge probably made a piss poor miscalculation. Who in his right mind wants to show up with a knife to a gunfight? Years later, my posture was greatly reinforced, but who knew way back then?

In the 1920s, keeping within the commonwealth's tight budget more than honoring tradition, we wore the exact same khaki uniform my papa did back in 1898, including the same leggings and campaign hats. We carried the same single-shot, Springfield Model 1873 rifle that my papa carried. It fired the .45-70 brass cartridge using black powder instead of smokeless powder. By comparison, the Regular Army was issued the M1903 Springfield rifle in .30-06 caliber. It's a five-shot, bolt-action rifle, with smokeless powder cartridges. The Regular Army used it to great effect during the Great War. Nevertheless, in spite of using an antique firearm, we felt like we were every bit as good as the militia our fathers had belonged to during the Spanish War.

I mustered into the militia in June of 1922 as a private. I mustered out three years later still as a private. It was the end of my term of enlistment. I received an honorable discharge from the newly formed National Guard Bureau instead of the Kentucky Militia. That didn't have much significance to anybody except for me until World War II rolled around.

-2-
Emancipation

I turned 21 in 1925 on the stroke of midnight between Saturday, February 28th and Sunday, March 1st, in that 1925 was not a leap year. I stood 5-feet, 10-inches tall in my stocking feet, and weighed 155 pounds in my underwear. I have blue eyes and short reddish-brown hair. By age 20 my beard grew like it was fertilized with horse manure, and shaving had become somewhat problematic for me. Have you ever tried to shave with a straight razor? It's a seriously hazardous undertaking! Being a thrifty Scot, I hated to pay my barber 10 cents every other day just to keep the bush whacked back, but I did on that particular day.

Now I was a fully emancipated, American male citizen. I could vote, handle my own financial affairs, enter into binding contracts, sue or be sued, buy or sell real estate, write a legal will, inherit property, get married, and legally possess alcohol except for now because of that stupid Volstead Act, otherwise known as Prohibition. From my observation, Prohibition was universally ignored by everyone except for the teetotalers and the Baptist ministers who didn't drink anyway. Of course, Scotsmen drank Scotch whiskey, but now being American and particularly a Kentuckian by choice, my papa switched to Kentucky bourbon. That's what all us boys drank. Papa liked Old Crow, named after the physician who first distilled it, so we did too. We never once considered ourselves outlaws for scoffing at and ignoring the ridiculous federal prohibition of alcohol. Most folks we knew felt the same as us.

Anyway, I knew exactly what I wanted to do with my life. I had known for a long time, but I had kept it all to myself.

Early Monday morning, the second day after my birthday, I went to work, except I waited outside the Office of the Mayor instead of reporting to my boss in the Message Room. He knew what I was doing anyway, because I told him what I planned to do before I left work Friday afternoon. He thought I had rocks in my head, but he was a swell guy and wished me well in my endeavor anyway.

Lucky for me, Mr. Mayor was kicking off the week with a slow, somnolent Monday morning. His secretary, Miss Alice Carpenter, recognized me. She told me to take a seat in his foyer and wait for him to acknowledge me. He met with two important citizens first. Then he stepped out of his office and looked at me. He asked, "Chester, who told you to come see me?"

"Nobody, Sir. I'm here on my own account to see you."

"Mr. Travis know about this?"

"Yes, Sir."

"Better come on in then and close the door. Then take a seat."

I'd been in his office many times, standing around waiting for him to sign something or send me off with some documents to hand deliver. This was the first time I had ever been invited to sit. It was auspicious.

"Okay, out with it. I'm a busy man if you hadn't noticed."

"Yes, Sir. Mayor Buschemeyer, I turned 21 on Sunday. I've worked here nearly three years, and during that time I've learned my way around both the City and County governments. I want to be a Louisville police officer, Sir."

"Oh for crying out loud, Chester! Do you even know how to shoot a gun?"

"Yes, Sir. I'm in the National Guard. I used to be in the Kentucky Militia, but things changed. I shot the equivalent of expert with the rifle twice in a row now. I never shot a revolver, but I'm certain I could learn to shoot it as good as a rifle."

"Okay, fine. What else you got going for you?"

"I graduated from High School in 1922."

"What else?"

"I'm not married. You know me. You know I'm a hard worker. I'll work hard; do whatever task I'm assigned to the best of my ability. I'm honest, loyal, and attend church each Sunday. I will be a great policeman if you hire me. That's my word, Sir. I won't let you down."

"You know how much a rookie patrolman makes, Chester?"

"Sir, as a matter of fact, I do. He makes 15 bucks a week. I make 10 now. It would be a 50% raise."

"You know you have to buy your own revolver and equipment? The city only pays for your uniforms - two pairs of trousers, one tunic, one hat, one overcoat. They replace 'em one for one if you wear 'em out, or get 'em torn up in a scuffle making an arrest."

"Yes, Sir."

"This is all learn as you go. We don't have a recruit school like they do in the big cities such as Chicago or New York. You learn the state laws and city ordinances by studying on your own. Also by following the instructions of your senior officers to a T. A policeman must be brave and possess the ability to figure out who's telling the truth and who's lying. He has to be fair and impartial. He has to be tough. Understand? Sometimes you have to fight, and if you lose you could die or be maimed for the rest of your life. You might get shot at or have to shoot and maybe even kill a hellbent lawbreaker. You really think you can measure up to all that? You're mighty young to be a cop."

"Yes, Sir."

"You know we have officers working on each shift, every day of the week. You'll work six days a week on whichever shift the Chief of Police assigns you to. By the way, do you know Chief Willard G. Hardin?"

"Yes, Sir."

"What's the word on Chief Hardin? Better tell it to me straight if you want the job."

"Sir, they say Chief Hardin's a hard-on."

"That's right. He's my hard-on. Get it?"

"Yes, Sir."

"Still want the job?"

"Yes, Sir."

"Hmmm. Chester, you register to vote yet?"

"I plan to do it today, Sir."

"What party do I belong to?"

"Democrat, Sir."

"Smart boy. Okay. I'll take a chance on you. You better not disappoint. Understand? I'm writing a message here telling Chief Hardin to hire you today as a patrolman 3rd grade. That's bottom of the totem pole. He'll tell you what to do next.

Before you do though, get down to the Board of Elections and get registered to vote. You better register Democrat. I'll be checking. If you foul up and get fired, I won't hire you back, not even as a messenger. I just decided to give that plum job to my nephew, but he ain't very smart and he'll probably fall flat on his face. Got it?"

"Yes, Sir."

"Okay. Best of luck. Take this (handing me an envelope with a handwritten note in it) to Chief Hardin. Off with you."

"Yes, Sir. Thank you. You won't regret it."

"Go!"

I ran down to the Board of Elections office and registered as a Democrat. Good thing I brought my birth certificate with me to prove I was 21, because I looked younger. I didn't wear any facial hair then. Not as easy to register to vote as I thought it would be.

Then I ran across the street to the Louisville Police Department Headquarters. I spoke with the clerk outside the Office of the Chief of Police. Her name was Iris Compton. She told me to wait in his foyer until he called me, but I didn't have to wait. He saw me and motioned for me to step inside his office.

He asked, "What have you got for me today, Chester?"

I handed him the envelope. He opened it and read it quickly. Then he looked up and asked, "Is this a joke? The mayor wrote for me to hire you. There must be a mistake. You ain't old enough to be a cop."

"No joke, Sir. I'm 21."

"Humph! You or your daddy and the mayor must be tight. You pals with the mayor, boy?"

"No, Sir."

"Likely story. You'll never last a week." He scribbled something on the note, put it in the envelope and handed it back. He said, "Take this to Personnel. Then report to Captain Nobles. You know who that is?"

"Yes, Sir. He's Captain of Patrol."

"Get the lead out, Sinclair! I just gave you an order."

"Yes, Sir. Thank you." I scrambled out of his office and his glaring countenance. He really was a hard-on, in fact, a gold plated one, at that.

The Federal Government passed the Civil Service Act in 1913. It effectively eliminated the spoils system for anyone below a cabinet level appointee in the Federal Government. The idea was to be fair in the hiring process, and to provide some sort of job protection to Federal employees. Under the new law, a Federal department head could no longer fire an employee without cause, or because he belonged to a different political party than the elected officials.

Similar legislation trickled down to the states. It hadn't made it to the City of Louisville yet. Otherwise, I would have had to apply through a formal vetting system to become a police officer. I knew all of this, more or less. I knew here under the political spoils system, I could be fired as easily as I was hired. I prayed that Chief Hardin viewed me as under the protection of Mayor Buschemeyer, at least long enough for me to be recognized as an asset and not a weak sister. Time would tell.

I went to Personnel. City Deputy Clerk Conrad Lincoln pulled my file. He annotated my resignation this date as a messenger. Then he annotated my appointment as a patrolman third grade. He also annotated my raise to $15 per week. He wrote a note on the mayor's letter and sent me and the letter to Captain Jonas M. (for Mighty they all said) Nobles.

Captain Nobles looked me over like I was an unidentified insect under a microscope. He said, "Sinclair, the Police Department can always use a good man. Are you a good man?"

"Yes, Sir."

"I hope for both our sakes you are. You're the first new man we've hired this year. I'm gonna do you the same way as I did Patrolman Wilkins when he came on last November. I'm starting you on Day Shift so I can keep my eye on you. You'll replace Bradley Wilkins beginning tomorrow. He's going to Night Shift tomorrow. I want to see your progress for myself. Once I see you know what you're doing and how you handle yourself, I'll reassign you too. Are we clear? You have to prove yourself to me first."

"Yes, Sir."

"Good. Now I'm going to swear you in." He called out to Patrolman Buford Atkins, his personal assistant. "Buford, bring me an Oath of Office form."

Buford brought the form. He dated it and wrote my full name in the blank at the top of the page. He passed it to Captain Nobles, who stood. He told me to stand and place my left hand on the Bible he pulled out from a drawer. He raised his right hand so I raised mine. I'd gone through a similar ritual when I joined the militia. He said, "Repeat after me."

"I, Chester Arnold Sinclair, do solemnly swear to uphold and defend the Constitutions of United States of America and the Commonwealth of Kentucky, its statutes, and the ordinances of the City of Louisville, fairly and impartially to the best of my ability, so help me God."

Then he showed me where to sign. Then Patrolman Atkins and Captain Nobles signed as witnesses. Atkins said, "I'll take this and the mayor's letter and have Conrad place them in his file."

He left, but returned two minutes later. He handed Captain Nobles a small, flat, blue cardboard box and two cards. Then he left again.

Captain Nobles handed me the cards and told me to sign them both. I did. Then he countersigned the first and returned it to me. It was a professionally printed, thick, high-grade, wallet-size, official Louisville Police Department identification card, bearing my first name, middle initial, and surname typed on the blank line across the middle. It confirmed my identity as a patrolman for anyone who chose to question it.

The second was a receipt for a badge and hat shield, both number 123, which were in the small box, which he opened and handed to me. Both were nickel-plated, heavy, and very shiny. He shook my hand and said, "Congratulations, Patrolman 3rd Grade Chester A. Sinclair. Welcome aboard.

"Last stop for you in Headquarters is the Supply Office, Second Floor, Room 204. Go see Patrolman Gilbert Dobbins and give him this note. Tell him I said for him to outfit you. Make sure everything fits properly - hat, overcoat, tunic, and two pairs of trousers.

"I'll be inspecting you tomorrow and you better look strack. Polished shoes or boots, close shave, neatly combed hair. Mustaches are okay so long as they are neatly trimmed. Better become best friends with your barber. Clean and neatly trimmed fingernails, too. It goes without saying your firearm better be spotless, fully functional, and loaded with fresh ammo. No tarnished cartridges. No damaged bullets. Got it?"

"Yes, Sir."

"Then go to Gabe's Pawn shop at 113 South Preston Street. This will hurt because it's going to cost you some jingle. If you don't have the cash, Gabe will open an account for you. He knows you're good for it because we don't retain deadbeat cops.

"You need a revolver in good repair, appropriate holster, box of ammo, serviceable pair of handcuffs, and billyclub. Altogether that's about $40.

"If you don't have a belt sturdy enough to support the weight of your gun and holster, you can buy one there. Your everyday suspenders will hold up your trousers. You also need comfortable, plain-toed black shoes or boots if you don't already own a pair. You're going to be on your feet a lot. Make sure your footwear fits properly and is comfortable or you won't last a week.

"Gabe has anything an officer could ever need to do his job, and he will try to sell it all to you. A lot of it is nice-to-have, not have-to-have. I told you what you have-to-have except for a pencil and a pocket notebook. I noticed that you do have a fountain pen, but you may not want to carry it day to day. A pen is nice, but not have-to-have (back in the day when there were just two types - straight pens for writing at a desk or table, which had to be dipped in an inkwell about every five words, or capped fountain pens you could put in your shirt pocket, but cost quite a bit more money. Many had nibs and clips made out of gold. Most blue collar men did not carry one.)

"Always wear your badge on your outer garment. Make sure your tunic and overcoat are loose enough to wear over your gun. Speaking of guns, many officers prefer cross-draw holsters. Try 'em both. See which you like best. There are several styles to choose from.

"Report for duty, armed and in uniform, not later than 0745 tomorrow morning. Don't forget to bring a padlock for your locker. Any questions?"

"Who do I report to, Captain?"

"Patrol Sergeant Julius Heim."

"Will do. Thank you, Sir."

As I was being fitted for my uniforms, things began to fall into place. Patrolman Dobbins was kind and a repository of need-to-know police customs and procedures.

The fabric on everything was a dark blue wool, but not navy blue. The trousers had straight legs without cuffs and were deliberately fitted a little loose around the waist 'for growth and comfort'. Like most trousers, they had inside-the-waistband buttons to fasten galluses, braces, suspenders, whatever you want to call them. Fortunately for me, I already owned two pairs, since they were not furnished. The trousers also had seven 1-1/2-inch loops around the waist to secure the gun belt.

Besides undergarments, officers were expected to wear a long-sleeve white cotton shirt. Fortunately, it wasn't necessary to wear the button-on celluloid collar, because the tunic fit high on the neck and completely concealed the shirt.

The tunic had a standard fold-down collar, not the stiff vertical collar sewn on some dress military uniforms (which choke the wearer to death). It had seven brass buttons in a single row down the front. All the buttons were embossed with the letters KY inside a semi-circular wreath. They were exactly like the buttons on my National Guard tunic. The tunic was cut with a loose fit around the middle to leave room for the sidearm and any other necessary accouterments an officer might want to wear on his belt. Another feature was vertical slash pockets waist high, which had an opening within so one could reach inside to retrieve his revolver, no matter which side it was worn.

The topcoat also fit loosely. It was very thick and extended down to three inches above the ground. It had the same single row of buttons down the front. It, too, had the vertical slit pockets with the interior opening. The inside was padded with quilting, and certainly designed for warmth during a bitterly cold winter night. It weighed about six pounds.

Both coats had a 2-inch long, 1/2-inch wide vertical strap with two metal grommets sewn on the left breast so the badge could be pinned to it without puncturing holes in the fabric.

The cap was made of the same wool as the garments. It had a round crown, and looked similar to the caps worn by the French military or some big city fire departments. It was vertical on the side instead of being saucer-shaped like they are today. The bill was made of black leather. It had an adjustable leather chin strap above the bill, fastened with a smaller screw-in version of the brass buttons on the coats. In addition, it had two vertical metal grommets on the front of the crown to fasten the hat shield.

I was impressed. My police uniforms put my National Guard uniforms to shame.

I took a few moments to study the badge and hat shield carefully. The badge was about 2-1/2 inches tall. It was shaped like a shield the knights of old used to protect themselves in combat. Louisville Police Department was scrolled across the top. My badge number, 123, was in the middle. KY was centered near the bottom. It had ornamental curly cues throughout.

The hat shield said Louisville Police Department in a semi-circle, reading left to right and open at the bottom. A depiction of the front of City Hall was in the middle. My badge number, 123, was beneath City Hall and KY was beneath that.

Now all I had to do was figure out a way to carry my uniforms home. Gilbert Dobbins foresaw this need and loaned me a Navy seabag, which I promised to return the next day. Then I walked the six blocks to Gabe's Pawn Shop. Soon as he laid eyes on me, he knew I was a new fish.

Gabriel G. Goldstein was in his mid-60s. His father had been a bartender, a drunk, and an incorrigible gambler. His mother turned tricks until she died of tuberculosis. Gabe was the oldest of three snot-nosed kids. He quit school in the 3rd grade, and at age nine began earning a living hustling bets for the bookies during the horse racing season. Then he added baseball season. He also sold newspapers and shined shoes and cleaned cuspidors in the saloons. He ran errands for merchants and anyone else who would pay him. He did whatever he needed to do to feed himself and his little brother and sister. He was responsible, and he worked hard.

At age 13, he was hired by another Hebrew, a shrewd, ancient Member of the Tribe, named Cornelius Liebowicz, who had no family to assist him in his pawn shop. Cornelius died ten years later at the age of 91. He willed his estate, consisting mostly of his pawn shop, which had living quarters on the second floor, to Gabe. Reliable Pawn Shop morphed into Gabe's. From that day forward, Gabe and his brother and sister never had another financial worry. Gabe was a natural-born businessman.

"Come in my good man! I bet Captain Nobles sent you to see me. Call me Gabe. I guarantee I have everything you need at the best price in town. What should I call you?"

"My name is Chester Sinclair, Sir. I live over at 718 South Floyd. I've walked by here many a time but never ventured inside. Never had anything I needed to pawn. You're right. Captain Nobles did tell me to come see you."

"Of course, he did. I thought so. Be glad to assist, but Chester, come see me anytime. You don't need to pawn anything. Truth is, I sell far more stuff than I take in pawn. I bet the first order of business is a revolver. Am I right?"

"Yes, Sir."

"Please, call me Gabe. Come over here and look in these two display cases. The one on your left contains used firearms. They're all in top notch condition or I wouldn't have them. The case on your right contains new firearms. The better firearms, Smith & Wesson and Colt are on the top and middle shelves. The cheaper revolvers, Harrington & Richardson (H&R), Iver Johnson, Webley, and a few other cheaper foreign makes are on the bottom.

"Just so you know, every officer I've ever sold a gun to

bought either a Colt or a Smith except for one. He bought an H&R, which is a reputable firearm, except the trigger pull is a mite stiff and it takes just a little more time to reload.

"Take your time. Let me know if you want me to get anything out so you can handle it. See how it feels in your hand."

I looked at several. I finally decided on a new, blue steel, Colt Police Positive Revolver with checkered walnut grips and a four-inch barrel, in .38 New Colt Police caliber. I also purchased two boxes of Western brand, 158-grain, lead round-nose bullets with a muzzle velocity of 767 feet per second and 206 foot-pounds of energy. It said so on the box.

I almost bought the very same model in the .32 New Colt Police caliber, which shot a 98-grain, lead round-nose bullet with a muzzle velocity of 718 feet per second and 112 foot-pounds of energy. The price for either gun was the same at $28, as was the price of ammo at $1.50 per box of 50; however, the projectile of the .38 was 50% bigger and nearly doubled the foot-pounds of energy, otherwise known as knockdown power, compared with the .32. Once Gabe pointed all this out to me, it was a no-brainer. Even so, he said most officers opted for the .32. He said he couldn't understand it.

I also bought a black leather, right-draw holster which had a very deep pocket, meaning the revolver went all the way down into the holster, leaving only the butt of the gun exposed. That eliminated the need for a protective strap to keep the gun from accidentally falling out. The cost was a mere two bucks.

For this purchase, Gabe saved me once again. I actually preferred a cross-draw, but he explained that it was hard enough to draw the gun from the right side (being right-handed), through the tunic pocket without getting the hammer spur snagged. Drawing cross-draw, one pulled the pistol all across his midsection, then through the tunic pocket, adding extra distance and more opportunities to get the hammer spur snagged; further, the draw was compounded even more if one were wearing an overcoat, especially if he had on gloves. Wanna be snazzy or wanna be quicker with fewer complications? It was another no-brainer.

Some might ask. Why not file off the hammer spur to eliminate snags?

Answer. Because then the revolver cannot be fired single action, which increases accuracy significantly, IF one has the time.

Gabe predicted that someday police departments would allow their officers to wear their revolvers out in the open and dispense with all this concealment nonsense, at least for their uniformed officers. "For Christ's sake - no discourtesy intended to you goyims [Gentiles] - the citizenry expects cops to be armed to protect themselves and the public. Why make officer safety less safe by going through this charade of concealing his gun? It defies logic. Nevertheless kid, this is the hand you've been dealt. Gotta work things out best you can to shade the odds of a gunfight more to your advantage." I listened carefully and learned much from this Jewish sage.

Continuing on my spending spree, I bought a gun cleaning kit for a buck. It included the machine oil, patches, and Hoppes #9 gun solvent. I purchased a black leather, 12-loop .38 caliber cartridge belt slide for another buck; also, a nickel-plated pair of Peerless handcuffs with two keys for two bucks; a packet of 10 police pocket notebooks with a pair of yellow number two lead pencils for 50 cents; a metal flashlight with two D-cell batteries on sale for a buck; and, a pair of Florsheim black leather boots with rubberized soles and cushioning on the inside for four bucks. (This was an extravagance, I knew, but they would last for several years.)

There were a lot more things I could have purchased, but I exercised restraint. Ha! Altogether, I shelled out $43.50 of my hard-earned cash. Might as well say three week's wages. I put everything in the sea bag and strolled home. I didn't have a helluva lot of cash left. I was down to $33 until payday. At least I didn't have to open a charge account with Gabe.

Mama looked up as soon as I crossed the threshold at the front door. She was getting ready to hang the wash outside on the clotheslines in the backyard. She wanted to see what I had in the seabag, so I dumped everything out on the couch. Then I showed her my badge.

She exclaimed, "Oh Chester! What have you gone and done? Are you trying to get yourself killed, Sweetie? I already have one son at sea in the Pacific Ocean who might as well be dead because he's never come home and it's been nearly six years. He seldom ever posts a letter, and if he did, where would I mail a response? When would he get it? He's always at sea.

"And now you? What will your papa say? You had such a good job! Why did you do this? Wasn't the Militia dangerous enough to suit you? Oh, dear, merciful God!"

Then she burst into tears, so I rushed to her side and hugged her. When she calmed down, I said, "Mama. I'm 21 years old now. I'm a full-grown man. This is what I want to be - a policeman. I want to help folks. Put bad guys in jail right here in Louisville. I'm not going anywhere. Assuming we don't get activated, my time in the National Guard will be up in three more months. Then you won't have to worry about that ever again.

"Besides, not that many cops get shot, Mama. When was the last one - Officer Tinsley three years ago? He was unlucky. He got shot in the back by a robber coming out of a drug store that sells more liquor than aspirin. He didn't even see the guy. It was just his bad luck. It could happen to anybody who's in the wrong place at the wrong time.

"I'm starting out on Day Shift tomorrow. Most of the action happens on the Afternoon Shift. They call it Swing Shift. I'll be careful. You know I will. I'm always careful. I'll still see you everyday unless you and Papa kick me out of the house for being a patriot. Do you want me to move away?"

"Heaven forbid! I want you to be safe! You're my baby. My last child. You've grown up too fast. You all have." Then the waterworks started again.

"Mama, you didn't think Junior or Phoebe grew up too fast."

"That's because they gave me grandbabies. Claude never will, but if he did I'd never see it. Ted and Abigail just got engaged. It will take them awhile. You don't even have a sweetheart yet, but you want to rush out and fight drunks and wife-beaters and arrest bank robbers and liquor store bandits!"

"Yes. I want to help folks who need the help. I want to put the predators behind bars. I need to do this. It's what I want. Understand? It's who I am. Who I'm meant to be - the White

Knight in shining armor. I hoped you would understand."

"I do understand, and that's what scares the dickens out of me. I know you won't back down, won't flinch, and that might just be the end of you. I pray for my husband and all my children everyday, asking God to protect them. Now I hafta double up on my prayers for you.

"Go put your gear away. Papa won't be home until Friday. He's on a swing to New Orleans. Promised to bring back some pralines. It's just you and me for supper tonight. We're having corned beef, mashed potatoes and gravy, biscuits, and applesauce. Let me know if I need to take any tucks or sew on any buttons at suppertime. I'll be out back hanging the wash. Also, before you get bogged down, get the leash and take Oscar for a walk. He needs the exercise, and for goodness sake, don't let him pee on Mrs. Goetz's bushes. She's still mad over the last time."

"Okay, Mama."

-3-
Learning 'The Job'

I got up at 5:30 the next morning to do my chores around the house before I left for work. First order of business was taking Oscar for a walk. When I returned, I brought in the newspaper from the front porch and put it on the end table next to Mama's rocker in the parlor. Next I brought more coal in for the pot belly stove in the parlor and the oven in the kitchen. I took a sponge bath in the washroom. Finally, I got dressed in my uniform, minus the topcoat, which I decided to leave at home, the temperature being 42 degrees with sunny skies. I had already tried on my uniform and new boots the evening before to ensure everything, particularly the gun belt, fit properly. It did. I had also put three coats of polish on my new boots. I looked almost as strack as I could, pending a shave.

Mama was already up preparing breakfast. We had coffee, fried eggs, grits, patty sausage, biscuits, and canned prunes (to regulate our bowels). In another month or six weeks we would have fresh strawberries. Mama said, "Chester, you truly are striking in your new uniform." She smiled, and gave me a big hug and a kiss on my cheek before I stepped out the door for the very first time to slay dragons and to save damsels in distress.

First stop was Carrot Top Scott's barber shop. With my beard growing as it fast as it does, I couldn't go two days without a shave like most men and look as strack as Captain

Nobles expected; however, I did decide to begin growing a mustache. A half hour later and ten cents poorer, I set out for Police Headquarters, trying to break in my new boots along the way. I felt conspicuous in my police uniform, just like I did the first few times I wore my uniform for the Militia. I arrived at 7:40, five minutes before I was told to report. I walked into the assembly room pretending it was old hat and I was perfectly at ease, which I was anything but.

Captain Nobles and Sergeant Heim were both there, along with eight or nine patrolmen having a gabfest amongst themselves, smoking and joking. Captain Nobles introduced me to Sergeant Heim, who was a mountain of a man, standing 6-feet, 4-inches tall, and weighing in at a trim 210 or 220 pounds. He was about 40 years old, with blond hair and a bushy walrus mustache. He was adorned with the highly coveted, silver Police Revolver Expert Badge pinned underneath his gold-plated Police Sergeant's Badge. (One day I hoped to become a police revolver expert.) He wore three, bright gold chevrons (with the points at the bottom like the letter V) on both sleeves of his tunic, and three gold hash marks on the bottom of his left sleeve, signifying at least 15 years of service.

Sergeant Heim shook my hand with a firm grip like he was squeezing the life out of a pesky varmint - maybe a rattlesnake but how would you know for sure?

He cracked a wide grin and said, "Glad to have you Sinclair. We've been a man short for awhile now. When we fall in for muster, you take your place at the right end of the row facing the podium. I'll introduce you to the platoon. Doubtful you'll remember many names, but it'll be a start.

Listen up, pay attention, and do what the other patrolmen do. Savvy?"

"Savvy, Sergeant."

"Good. We have a few minutes. If you're not too shy, you might want to join the other patrolmen and mix and mingle."

"Yes, Sergeant."

I did what he suggested. Most of the men were friendly. One or two were not. I did my best to put names with faces. We didn't wear name tags in those days so it was a challenge, but I did remember some. More patrolmen trickled in. Including myself, I counted 14.

The clock on the wall reflected it was 8 o'clock. Sergeant Heim took his place behind the podium. Captain Nobles took up a position in front along the wall facing the men. Sergeant Heim bellowed, "Fall in, ladies. Eyes straight ahead facing me." We all fell in. It was just like being in the National Guard, the very same.

Sergeant Heim called roll. I could tell he was proceeding down the line from his left to right. Every cog in its place. I figured it had something to do with seniority since the names he called out were not in alphabetical order.

He called me front and center and told me to face the platoon. I did. He introduced me, saying I came highly recommended. I was thankful he didn't mentioned that the high referral came from Hizzoner, Mayor Buschemeyer, himself. Then I was instructed to fall back in.

We started with an inspection from the other end. As the sergeant proceeded down the line, the occasional patrolman was instructed to retrieve his revolver, open the cylinder, dump the cartridges into his hand, and present the empty gun for examination. Others were not, but I could see what was coming. When it was my turn, I was told to do likewise. I did. Sergeant Heim examined my spanking new Colt and my cartridges and handed them back. He said, "Excellent choice, Sinclair." I reloaded and reholstered. Then he returned to the podium and told everyone to take out his notebook. Fortunately, I had discovered that the left inside breast of the tunic had a pocket just for that purpose.

Sergeant Heim called out the day's assignments. "Welch, Desk; Roberts and Ernhardt, Beat 1; Campbell and O'Toole, Beat 2; Rizzo and McArthur, Beat 3; Constantine and Davis, Beat 4; Hopewell, Beat 5; Llewellyn, Beats 6 and 7; Caldwell, Beat 8; Bishop and Sinclair, Paddy Wagon. (They call it a paddy wagon because in the bad old days they arrested a lot of Irish for drunk and disorderly. The slang term for Irish was paddy, probably a derivative for Patrick.)

"Listen up. Last night we had a break-in by parties unknown at Warren's Hardware, located at 6th and Vine. At least 16 revolvers and two shotguns were stolen, including ammo. Be extra vigilant when approaching suspects. You never know what they're carrying these days, especially now. If you get any leads, pass them along to Detective Ogilvie.

"Also, around midnight the West End Social Club, a well-known speakeasy at 32nd and Potter, in the roughest section of the West End, was held up by three Negro males, two armed with revolvers and one with a single-shot shotgun. Robbers got away with an undetermined amount of cash, meaning hundreds of bucks, in 1s, 2s, 5s, and 10s. Probably not many 20s floating around there. They also probably scooped up all the silver, too.

"You all know that joint is a dive with a multitude of unsavory patrons, many of whom are armed, so it's a wonder no one was shot or stabbed. Indications are, they had several high stakes poker games going on at the time. Robbers got away in a Model T Ford driven by a fat Negro broad wearing a floppy white hat.

"The perps are all described as medium height, slender build, and dark-complected; however, the one dressed in a brown pinstripe suit with brown and white wingtips had a gold tooth in front. That matches the description of Willie Joe Jefferson, 33 years of age. He's a shifty scoundrel, last known address at 31st and Chestnut in the Carillon Arms Apartments. He's got two priors - one for armed robbery and the other for felon in possession of a firearm. Did two stints in the joint.

"Jefferson's known associates are Sleepy John Williams, 26 years of age, with a pencil-thin mustache like Clark Gable. Last known residence was with his mama, Bernice Epps, at 3133 North Winston. He's got two priors for B&E (breaking an entering), for which he served four years in Eddyville.

"Next is LeRoy "Sticks" Jones, Jr., 31 years of age, snappy dresser, usually has a thick gold chain hanging between his vest pockets, wears a bright green suit, always wears spats, and a beige fedora with a green parrot feather in the hat band. Several priors for illegal gambling, disorderly conduct, possession of non tax-paid alcohol, carrying a concealed deadly weapon, indecent exposure, and so forth, but no felony convictions. Known to carry an ice pick strapped to the inside of his left calf, so if you find him beware.

"Right now these sterling citizens are just suspects, not

fugitives. They haven't been positively IDed yet. Detectives are out beating the bushes looking for them as we speak. I have mugshots of all these characters. After roll call, come up and take a gander unless you already know 'em on sight. I know some of you do.

"That's it. Be timely with your hourly call-ins. Motorized units remember to check the oil and top off with fuel at end of shift. Also, make sure the garage is aware of any damage which you noticed prior to your shift, and let them know about any repairs or servicing which needs to be done. Failure to do so will result in your return to foot patrol. It's not like the department has a fleet of extra machines just waiting for you all to tear up. Okay. Get to it. Dismissed."

I looked over at the patrolman standing next to me. He was a wizened old guy, about 70 (could be older), 5-feet, 5-inches tall, 120 pounds (maybe), bushy white hair and eyebrows, and Wyatt Earp mustache. His tunic had nine white hashmarks on his left sleeve, signifying at least 45 years of service, meaning he came on by 1880, if not before. He was busy lighting up a corncob pipe. I asked, "Are you Patrolman Bishop?"

"Right you are. Patrolman First Grade Oliver T. Bishop at your service. The T stands for Truman. You can call me Oliver. Suits me just fine. I'm the most senior officer in this whole dern department. I j'ined up oncet I got out of the Army in 1877 right after I turned 21. I was a private in the 7th Cavalry during the Battle of the Little Big Horn. Served under Major Marcus Reno. He was breveted to Brigadier General during the War Between the States, but when I was under his command, he was a major. He was one brave son of a bitch, too. I was borned right here in Louisville in 1856. I growed up during the Yankee occupation. Always hated them dern Yankees, but I j'ined 'em anyway in 1873 when I turned 17, because I wanted to be an Indian fighter and the Confederacy was no more. My mama almost disowned me but she didn't. Now tell me a little about yourself, Sinclair."

I extended my hand. We shook and I said, "Honored to know you, Oliver. I don't have any of your experience, but I do belong to the National Guard. It was called the Kentucky Militia when I first joined. I grew up in Louisville, too. I was 13 when the Great War commenced, but I can't say we were ever inconvenienced. Before I was born, my papa joined the 1st Kentucky Volunteer Infantry Regiment in the Militia during the Spanish War. They were only in country a few days before the Spanish threw up the white flag. He's an engineer on the L&N. I got three brothers and one sister, all older. I'm the only one still at home, living with Mama and Papa. I joined the police department yesterday at age 21 just like you. That pretty much sums me up."

"Tell you what, Chester. You hurry over and study the mugshots of those three colored robbers before we head out. Sarge'll be pissed off if you don't, but you need to do it anyway so's you can learn how to memorize faces. See anything noteworthy, jot it down in your notebook next to the date, name, and why he's wanted along with any other helpful information such as he always wears a green parrot feather in the hatband of his beige fedora. The reason is, if you was walking home at end of shift and happened to recognize one of 'em and put the grabbola on him, you'd be a hero overnight. The brass would figger you knew your job and leave you alone to go do it without standing over your shoulder. Life would be better for you instantly. Got it?"

"Got it. Be right back."

I rushed over and had all the time I needed to study the mugshots. The other patrolmen had moved on.

Willie Joe Jefferson's right front tooth was the one with the gold cap. He had one of those little triangular beards just below his lower lip like a lot of Negroes do. He had a small vertical scar on his left eyebrow in the middle.

Sleepy John Williams had wide, flared nostrils like a scared horse. His ears were tiny, like possum ears. That was all I could see remarkable about him except for his Clark Gable mustache.

LeRoy 'Sticks' Jones, Jr. had a look of supreme confidence like he had mastered life. His flare for clothing would always give him away. The only distinctive facial feature I could see were his ears, which were on the large side, pointy at the bottom, and stuck out a little too far from his head.

Oliver was dead-bang right. I noticed Sergeant Heim watching me very closely to see to what degree I studied the mugshots and made notes. He seemed satisfied.

Note to self: Always take diligent notes on suspects if for no other reason than to keep Sarge off your back.

I walked back over to Oliver and said, "Ready to go when ever you are. Sorry to keep you waiting. What do we do next?"

"We ain't in no big hurry, Chester. Take a leak if you need to; otherwise, follow me to the stable. We still use a double mule team to draw the paddy wagon. We ain't never in no hurry. Cap'n Nobles would rather have another automobile for patrol than a panel truck to haul prisoners. Mules is all they've ever used here to haul prisoners, and personally, I think mules is less cantankerous than gasoline-propelled machines. You ever driven a machine?"

"Nope. How long you been on the paddy wagon?"

"Oh, about ten years. They usually give it to the old guys. In my younger days, at one time or another, I patrolled every dern beat in this city. Naturally, I preferred some over others. Did it for more'n 30 years.

"Now with some age and a little seasoning behind me, I prefer the paddy wagon. This is why. Between hauling prisoners to and fro, I can wander anywhere I want within the city limits. Besides, if I see someone who needs locking up, I still tend to business. You don't have to be no beat cop to hook up a scalawag. That's why we all carry the same size badge and tote a gun of our own choosing.

"The main difference betwixt a beat cop and the paddy wagon man is, I don't get orders from the callbox to take a report of a crime, or perform a passel of other braindead tasks which have nothing whatsoever to do with enforcing the law. A citizen needs some kind of nonsense assistance, and the city don't know who else to send, so they send the beat cop.

"Take this for example. One time I got a call to go see an old widow woman who needed help but they didn't say what, so I hurried right on over. Poor thing. She couldn't help it. She was batshit crazy and didn't have no kith nor kin nearby. She thought ghosts was hiding under her bed. Convinced of it. Couldn't get her to calm down. Scared to death.

"Finally, I asks if she had a broom. She did. She fetched it for me, so I got down on my hands and knees and yelled at the ghosts under the bed and said I was gonna murderlize 'em if they didn't get out of the house. I swept under the bed, making a big racket. Finally, I got 'em all. I swept 'em to the parlor. I told her to hurry up and open the door. She did, and I swept 'em off the porch and said they better never come back if they knew what was good for 'em. They all vamoosed into the bright sunshine, but you couldn't see 'em. I told her they was gone never to come back, but she should keep her doors locked anyway in case they changed their minds. She was pleased as punch, and I went on my merry way. Fortunately, she never had any other problems, at least so far as I know of.

"That is one of the primary jobs of a beat cop. Pacify those what need pacifying. Got it?"

"That's a hoot. What a job! Yes, Sir. Lesson learned."

"Today, they mostly call me to pick up arrestees. Maybe run an errand for the Cap'n, but usually not. It makes no never mind to me. I still get paid either way. You'll understand what I'm talking about oncet they assign you to a beat, which will probably be Beat 8 which is all colored. If you ain't had much to do with coloreds, you soon will. Different breed of cat. People is people, all with the same basic needs, but they's just like the Irish. They all love to fight. The difference is, the Negroes seem to fornicate more and they don't care whose wife they do it with. That's what causes most of the altercations.

"Another thing. Sad to say, but today some of our patrolmen ain't exactly what I'd call go-getters. Believe it or not, I make more arrests than half the patrol officers, yet I haul every prisoner arrested during Day Shift to jail. Chester, what I mean to say is, you can decide to be as big or as little as you want. It's up to you.

"By the way, you ready to get to work? We got some prisoners in our lock-up what need to go to the Jefferson County Jail, and maybe one or two what need to go from there to here."

"Absolutely, but first can you teach me how to rig up a team of mules? I've never been around mules or horses much, but I'm anxious to learn."

"Come on, city slicker. It's high time you got an education on mules. Ornery as they can be, but the best beast God ever put on Earth."

Oliver introduced me to all six of the mules owned by the police department. He called them all by name and stroked their muzzles. Today we took out Samson and Delilah. I learned how to harness a team without any help. It wasn't as hard as I thought.

Afterwards, we walked up to the third (and top) floor of HQ to the Louisville City Jail. I learned how to pat down a prisoner for weapons or contraband (which really means anything he isn't supposed to have, like a knife, chewing tobacco - roll-your-own smokes were okay - or ladies' undergarments for example). We had three. Then I learned how to handcuff a prisoner the correct way. We put leg irons and handcuffs on all three mutts because they were charged with felonies, which can only be tried in Jefferson County Circuit Court by Judge W.H. Davidson. He also tries all misdemeanors committed in Jefferson County outside of Louisville City Limits. Louisville City Court Judge Wendell R. Jamison can only try misdemeanors committed within the city limits.

The mutt named Howard Gruber was charged with beating his wife to death with a fireplace poker in a drunken fit of rage. He was a big, burley SOB with a bad attitude, so we saved him for last before taking him down the two flights of steps. He was facing execution by hanging if he got convicted, so we were extra vigilant when dealing with him. The other two were charged with non-violent crimes, burglary and grand larceny, so although we exercised caution, we were not as wary of them trying to escape.

I had my brand new, 14-inch, Osage orange (hedge apple) billyclub, known for its hardness and durability, in my hand. I noticed Oliver was not carrying his, so when we were alone I asked him why. He replied, "Chester, I been dealing with hard-cases all my life. You've done noticed I ain't a big feller, so at an early age I learned to size up folks real quick in the event they decided to do me harm, and I mean everyone I come into contact with. You never know what a scairt or angry man might do. Woman either. They all fall into three categories. Them I can handle with my bare hands; them what take a big stick to subdue; and them which I'd have to shoot. I've done all three.

"Edwards (the burglar) and O'Roark (the thief) are not a threat to me. I can handle them with my hands. Gruber is one I'd hafta shoot. That's why I carry a 1873 Colt Peacemaker with a 5-1/2-inch barrel in .45 Long Colt caliber. It shoots a 250-grain lead ball. I wear it in a cross-draw shoulder holster. Before I ever face someone like Gruber, I undo the two middle buttons of my tunic so's I can grab it fast. Also, the barrel's long enough to use it like a truncheon.

"If Gruber acted up while we was on the stairs, first option would be give him a shove, hoping he'd fall all the way down and break his neck. On level ground, I'd just plug him and turn his black heart into mincemeat. He's big and mean and a known killer. Believe me when I say the world would be better off without him. If'n it came to killing him, nary a soul would shed a tear. Besides, they's three reliable eyewitnesses testifying against him. He for sure done it. He's a dead man walking. Two months from now he'll be swinging from a gallows. If'n ya ain't never seen a hanging, it's high time ya did. I'll take ya. It's grim business, but it has to be done if justice is to prevail.

"This is why you're assigned to me. My job is to learn you how to do your job so you can go home at end of shift, safe and sound to your mama. Savvy?"

"Savvy. I appreciate everything you've taught me so far."

We dropped off the prisoners at the county jail without incident. They didn't have any prisoners for us to pick up, which is what Oliver expected. About the only time they ever do, is if an outstanding (misdemeanor) city warrant had been executed by a deputy sheriff.

When we were done, it was time for our first call to HQ, so we went to the nearest callbox. Oliver had me call in. They didn't have anything for us, so Oliver began taking me around the city to show me the beat boundaries, and point out the locations of all the other callboxes. He said if nobody made an arrest on our shift, we wouldn't have much to do. All the while, he explained different aspects of 'The Job' (police slang for police department) so I would not find myself 'flatfooted' out of ignorance.

After lunch at a greasy spoon, consisting of a fried bologna sandwich, bowl of pintos, canned peaches, and black coffee, all for 20 cents, we rode over to a vacant lot over on Beat 6 near the river. It had a partially demolished brick building. We stopped so I could practice shooting with a backstop, since I mentioned I hadn't had an opportunity to shoot my new gun.

It was obvious that a lot of shooters had been here before us. Someone had found an old wooden kitchen table that was used as a platform for tin cans, bottles, and other suitable targets. I hadn't expected this, so the only extra ammo I brought was what I had placed in my belt slide. We found plenty of tin cans with bullet holes. We selected the ones with the least amount of damage.

Initially, Oliver had me back up about five yards from the table. He examined my new Colt and proclaimed it to be first class.

He said, "With your experience shooting a rifle, this shouldn't be much of a transition. You already know how to center the front sight blade with the rear sight. The main thing you'll have to watch, is not to jerk the trigger when you shoot. If you do, being right-handed, your rounds will go low left.

"Also, most pistoleros shoot one-handed. In an emergency, especially in a close range shootout, you usually have to. However, you will have more accuracy if you shoot the gun two-handed. Getting the same grip on the butt each time you draw is also critical. Consider the pistol nothing more than an extension of your arm. Keep your wrist and elbow locked each time you fire. (He pulled his Colt and demonstrated everything he just said.)

"Today, I recommend you start out aiming for this big can

over here on your left (pointing to a 46-ounce tomato juice can). Take your time and fire one round."

I adjusted my feet, cocked, aimed, and fired. "Boom!" The round blew a sizable hole in the front near the middle of the can. It soared five feet in the air, landing on the ground. Oliver picked it up, and pointed to the half dollar-size hole in the back. He exclaimed, "Excellent! Try it on this 16-ounce can. See if you can hit in the middle, too."

The results were the same.

"Very good. Move back two yards and shoot this coffee can."

Ditto.

Ultimately, I moved back to ten yards to continue my training. All my shots were two-handed, carefully aimed, single action, and hit the mark. I was thrilled. I loaded my last six cartridges and reholstered. This was the highlight of my first day on the job. Oliver was more than satisfied with my performance. So was I.

This first week in March was slow. I purchased two more boxes of ammo. I didn't even wince at the cost. Oliver took me shooting each day except for one one when we were too busy transporting new arrestees. I felt like an old salt by the time Papa returned home Friday evening. By then, I was no longer self-conscious about wearing my uniform. It felt right and so did I.

Papa smiled when he saw me. He gave me a firm handshake and a slap on the back. He said, "Son, we are both very proud of you. Work hard. Be careful. Do what is right. Mama and I will do the rest and pray for your safety."

I spent nearly six months as Oliver's sidekick. Looking

back, it may have been my happiest six months on The Job. I learned what was expected and how to do it right. Oliver was a kind and patient teacher, and an all around good guy to be partnered with. He had been a widower for six years. Now he lived with a daughter named Eloise Carpenter and her husband, Harvey. Oliver's kids were all grown, but the grandkids were nearby and they all loved to visit Pappy.

Some months later, Captain Nobles transferred me to the Swing Shift on Beat 7. It was a walking beat on the east side of the downtown central business district (CBD). It had some tall buildings, but it also had a substantial residential section. In fact, Papa's house was on Beat 7. Many evenings I was able to eat supper at home.

Time passed slowly, or so I thought. Time is usually your friend when you are young and strong, virile and bulletproof, with plenty to spare.

-4-
Changes Good and Bad

Time passed quickly without my notice. I had fallen in love with The Job and couldn't imagine doing anything else for a livelihood. Whether by design or not, Captain Nobles assigned me a walking beat which included my own neighborhood. It was the only residence I had ever known. It was like throwing Br'er Rabbit into the briar patch. (See Uncle Remus for details.) I stayed on Swing Shift for three years before being transferred back to Day Shift.

The Louisville Police Department (LPD) went through several changes during the next four years. Being the new kid on the block, I had not gotten set in my ways yet - different from many of the old hands.

In 1926, the Department had an event which prompted change. The event itself was of paramount significance to me, but certainly not the end result. Patrolman Oliver T. Bishop passed away. He was 70 years old. They found him dead, sitting at the helm of the paddy wagon in front of the Jefferson County Courthouse. It looked like his ticker just gave out. No foul play suspected.

Oliver was well-known and beloved by all. His funeral was absolutely epic - bagpipes, Police and Army Honor Guards, 21-gun salute, burial at Zachary Taylor National Cemetery (limited to combat veterans), plus closing remarks by Hizzoner, Mayor John H. Buschemeyer. The powers that be even appropriated Oliver's paddy wagon, the only one the

Department owned, to function as his hearse. They did this in honor of him, and his 48 years of honorable and faithful service to the Louisville Police Department.

A short time later, after the dust had settled, they retired the mule-drawn paddy wagon. They stashed it out of sight (and long-term memory) in a city-owned warehouse. They sold all the mules, and bought a Diamond T truck to replace it. It made Oliver's replacement, Patrolman Hilliard C. "Fatso" Froggett extremely happy. He claimed he was better with machines than mules (or people for that matter.)

Different from Oliver, Fatso was not a credit to the Louisville Police Department. Nobody could remember the last time he made an arrest. He was a 58-year-old, 5-feet, 6-inch, 250-pound slug with bad breath and eye-watering body odor. He had survived on The Job for 22 inglorious years by hitching his hook to Chief Willard G. Hardin's star, back when he was still a patrol sergeant. Everyone else despised Fatso and did all they could to avoid him.

In those days, LPD only had six officers with supervisory rank. The chief was a major. Next in line was the captain of patrol. The detectives were commanded by a lieutenant. The three shifts were commanded by a patrol sergeant. Fatso ran then-Sergeant Hardin's errands, cut his grass, burned his trash, trimmed his bushes, washed his machine, painted his fence, and anything else he was asked to do. See, in any bureaucracy, especially LPD, there's always a place for a lackey. Now as paddy wagon man, Fatso had a gold-plated license to loaf, and he took full advantage. At least now, the prisoners and whichever unfortunate rookie drew the helper position on the paddy wagon, were the only ones who had to smell Fatso for more than just a few moments.

Then Time turned the page and it became 1927. This was an epic year for changes within our hide-bound police department.

Mayor Buschemeyer decided to modernize the style of our uniforms. The rumor mill suggested Hizzoner decided to do this because his father-in-law was the sales representative for the uniform supply company, and received a big fat commission. (Say it ain't so!) It was a major contract worth a bodacious boatload of money. With 20-20 hindsight, it was actually fortuitous the City decided to make this and the other transitions at this particular time while it was flush with taxpayer money. Two years hence it would have been an impossibility. Compared with other similar size police departments across the nation, we would have looked and been perceived as anachronistic.

The new issue for uniformed officers included baby blue, long sleeve shirts and a black necktie, which was to be tied in a Windsor knot. Sergeants and above received white shirts. The new trousers worn by patrolmen had baby blue piping along the outer seam of the legs. Rank had gold piping. The prevailing thought was that this was done to preclude officers from wearing their uniform trousers off-duty. Save the city some money on replacing trousers worn out due to wear and tear unrelated to the job.

The new tunic was similar in design to the Army's. Of course it was the same dark blue material as the trousers and cap. It had an open throat with lapels, and button-down, outside breast and side waist pockets with flaps (for a total of four). The tunics also had two inside breast pockets. The single row of buttons on the front were reduced from seven to five. Oddly, they added button-down epaulet straps on the shoulders, I suppose for looks. In that we didn't wear a diagonal leather shoulder strap (like the military), we didn't need the epaulet straps to hold anything down. They were just there. The design on the buttons remained the same as before, some say from as far back as the War Between the States. The rear coattail had a vertical vent, in contrast to the old tunics which had none. The vent made the tunics more comfortable when sitting down.

We kept the old topcoat. As a walking beat cop, I truly appreciated that. It was warm.

The new cap was also designed like Army's, with the crown looking more like a flying saucer (hence its nickname) instead of a short oval, flat-topped silo like the French gendarmes wear. Besides, everyone hated the old caps.

These were all welcome changes, but of no big consequence. However, there were two seismic changes in the uniform regulations.

Now, we wore our gun belts outside the tunic for easier access to our sidearms. That was a major step for officer safety and survival. Also, during warm weather, we eliminated the tunic altogether. We wore the badge on our shirt. At long last, the Department acknowledged it was too hot to wear a wool tunic in sweltering weather!

The new clothing issue included three pairs of wool trousers, six shirts, two ties, wool tunic, wool cap, and a 1-1/2-inch-wide black leather gun belt. This signaled the demise of shoulder holsters for patrolmen. We still wore suspenders to hold up our trousers when we wore the tunic. Otherwise, suspenders were replaced by our new gun belt, which was designed to hold up our trousers, and carry the weight of the holstered revolver, spare ammunition, handcuffs, and strap with a metal ring to secure our billyclub (when it wasn't in use). Without suspenders, if the officer had a flat ass (and many men do), his trousers were always sliding down due to the weight of his gear. He was forever pulling them up and tucking in his shirttails.

There was another significant change unrelated to uniforms. They added two more beats for a total of 10. Both Beats 6 and 7 were divided in half, north to south. The western half of Beat 6 became Beat 9. The eastern half of Beat 7 became Beat 10. The beats never were in strict numerical order, but this made it even worse. Nevertheless, they decided it would be too confusing to renumber them all. They'd had the same eight beats for nearly 30 years. Officers could assimilate the new beat boundaries fairly quickly - at least that was the reasoning.

Beats 6, 7, 9, and 10 were walking beats because for the most part, they comprised the central business district (CBD). To this end, the Department hired eight more officers, bringing the authorized strength up to 62, to include the position of Chief of Police.

Also in 1927, the Police Department created a Training Sergeant position. All new hires were put through a rigorous three-week training program by him before they were assigned to a beat (under the tutelage of a trusted experienced officer). He also conducted annual firearms training for all officers without exception. Failure to qualify annually was grounds for removal, although to my knowledge they never fired anyone for this. I loved the firearms training. It allowed me to shoot departmental ammo and earn the coveted Police Revolver Expert Badge like Patrol Sergeant Heim. In fact, we were the only two recipients on LPD.

A monumental change of lasting importance to every city employee also occurred in 1927. Louisville adopted a Civil Service program fashioned after the federal system. All civil servants including policemen were covered under its domain. It turned out to be a very good thing by providing greater job security, which became more and more important to me as I got older.

Finally, there was one other enormous, life-altering transition during this period, but it had absolutely nothing to do with The Job.

On Saturday afternoon, February 12th, 1927, while on my way to work, I stopped by the apothecary a couple of blocks from home. I went in to purchase a Valentine's Day card for my mama. I was waited upon by this stunning creature I had never before seen.

She had bright blue eyes, a peaches and cream complexion, and blond hair done up in a loose bun. She was slim and stood about 5-feet, 4-inches tall. Under all her garments, there was no way I could calculate her weight. Suffice it to say, I could tell she had round hips and a full bosom, both of which caught my attention. She was wearing a long sleeve, white cotton blouse with puffy sleeves and a pale green gathered skirt. I guessed correctly that she was 20 years of age.

She saw me looking at Valentine cards. I finally selected one. She said, "That card is especially nice. Officer, did you want to get a petite lacy hanky to put inside the envelope for your sweetheart?"

I replied, "Oh, it's for my mama. I don't have a sweetheart, but if I did, I hope she would be just like you. Yes, I would like to get Mama a lacy hanky. By the way, my name is Chester Sinclair. They call me Chet. I live in this neighborhood, but I've never seen you before. Do you mind if I ask your name, Miss?"

She blushed bright red like a bowl of fresh cherries, yet she was smiling. She was clearly embarrassed. Once she recovered and composed herself, she looked me right in the eye and replied, "Oh, I shouldn't have presumed, Officer Sinclair. My name is Chloe Svensen, and I just began working here a couple of weeks ago. My family recently moved to this neighborhood from Auburndale, where my grandparents own a small farm."

"Miss Chloe Svensen, I'm not an especially bashful person, but it seems that right now the cat's got my tongue. Please just call me Chet. Um, could you direct me over to the ladies' hankies?"

"Right over here. Does your mama have a passion for cats? Some of these have cats embroidered on them. They're quite striking."

"She does. In fact, we have a yellow and white tiger stripe named Sunshine. I like this one here, with the yellow cat and his big green eyes. It reminds me of him.

"Before you ring me up, would it be too bold of me to ask if you would like to go with me to Fountain Ferry Park tomorrow after church? We could walk down to the riverfront and take the steamboat. I promise to get you home by whatever time you need to return. If it weren't for the fact that I have to go to work right now, I would have asked you to accompany me to a motion picture tonight."

"Now you have presumed on me, Officer Sinclair. What if I said I had a beau?"

"Of course, you're absolutely right. It's my misfortune. The story of my life. I should have known a woman of your beauty and charm would already be spoken for. Please excuse my bad manners."

"Pshaw! I didn't say I had a beau. I said what if. As it turns out, I do not. I just wanted to see if I could get a rugged policeman such as yourself, Chet, to blush.

"Yes. I would love to go to Fountain Ferry Park with you. Stop by my house tomorrow at 12:30 to meet my folks. We live at 416 South Preston Street."

"Wonderful. We're practically neighbors. I most certainly will. What's your papa's name?"

"His name is Henry V. Svensen. He's a conductor on the L&N. He's intimidating to many people. He may try to scare you off. In fact, I bet he will."

"I'll be on my best behavior, although in my line of work, I encounter intimidating people quite a bit. And just so you know, my papa, Angus R. Sinclair, happens to work for the L&N. He's an engineer. My eldest brother, Junior, works there as a coalman. They may even know each other."

"My, my. Such a small world. Well, I'll tell my papa to be nice to you since he may know your papa or brother.

"Is there anything else I can get for you, Chet?"

"No. That's it. Thank you, Miss Chloe."

"All righty then. The total comes to 89 cents."

I paid.

She smiled brightly.

I said, "See you tomorrow at 12:30. Good day, Miss Svensen."

"Good day, Officer Sinclair."

I walked the rest of the way to work on Cloud 9. I couldn't get her off my mind.

The next morning at breakfast, I told my folks about my good fortune. Mama was ecstatic. Papa said he knew Henry Svensen and that he was a solid man. They both told me to be on my best behavior. I said they could count on it.

I wore my baseball letterman's sweater under my coat. It really impressed her papa and younger brother. It was a cool day with a slight breeze and a few fluffy clouds, but the sun shone brightly against a cobalt blue sky. It was a magical day, forever embedded in my memory. It ended much too soon. I was completely smitten, consumed, slain, and I had an inkling Chloe was too. I took her out on a date at least once every week, but most times twice. It just wasn't enough. I needed more.

I learned she graduated from Female High School in 1925. Her favorite subjects were English and Latin. Her least favorite was any math class subsequent to General Math.

She was passionate about playing the piano. She'd been taking lessons for 10 years. Her family belonged to the Lutheran Church. They attend most Sundays but not all. She wouldn't mind checking out some other denominations.

Her favorite color was yellow. She has one yellow dress which she wears for special occasions.

She has a gray and black striped tiger cat with four white socks. His name is Igor. He's a champion mouser.

She likes to dance. Once she drank a gin rickey. It's made with lime juice. She really liked it. Her folks don't know. Her papa prefers bourbon and her mother prefers red wine. They have bottles and bottles of blackberry wine her grandpa and grandma made on their farm in Auburndale. It's really good. Don't tell anyone.

Someday she'd like to take the train to New Orleans to see the Mardi Gras. It sounds like so much fun. Did I have an interest in going? Maybe sometime we could go together.

We connected with each other on every level. I couldn't imagine not seeing her as often as possible. I was pretty certain I'd found my soulmate.

Two months later I was invited to her house for supper. They served roast beef. I got closer acquainted with her papa, mama (Miss Janine), and younger brother, Percival, who was a senior at Male High School. He plays guard on the basketball team, and was hoping to earn a letter this year. He just missed it last year. It's been his dream. Her sisters Constance and Eliza, are already grown and married. They were not present, but I met them later on. Sweet ladies both.

A week after that, Mama invited Chloe's family to our house for supper. She served Southern fried chicken. Miss Janine brought a bottle of blackberry wine. Papa broke the seal on a bottle of Old Fitzgerald made right here in Louisville, which he picked up on a passenger stop in Bowling Green from a bootlegger he knows. Go figure! Nobody present had a kind word for Prohibition. It was like our families had known each other for decades.

Afterwards, Mama asked if I were ever going to ask Chloe for her hand in marriage. I said yes. She asked when. I said soon. She said I better get a move on or somebody else was liable to steal her away from me.

A month later I proposed and she said yes. I asked after we had a scrumptious meal at the Brown Hotel. What a relief and celebration! We set the date for Saturday, September 17th, at the Presbyterian Church.

It was then I suddenly realized I needed to buy a machine. Heck, I had never even driven one! Only rode in a police machine twice. I've always walked everywhere I needed to go. I even walk a foot beat by choice. Nevertheless, now I was engaged, the time had finally come. It was time to purchase an automobile. Being a Scotsman, I'd been thrifty all my life. I studied the advertisements in the *Courier Journal*. I wanted to get an idea of what it would cost. I had the cash, but I hated to part with it. Time to fish or cut bait. I decided to fish.

I walked down to the Broadway Ford dealership to see what he had for sale. The dealer, Mr. Grinstead, had a grand total of three Model Ts. They were all black, with him trying to convince me that black was the color most preferred by customers. Wait a minute! Didn't Henry Ford himself say the customer can buy any color Ford he wants so long as he wants black? Maybe Mr. Grinstead thought I just fell off a turnip truck. I thought I presented better than that. Guess I didn't.

At the time, I didn't know Ford had decided not to make anymore Model Ts after this year. I kinda doubt the dealer did either. All I knew was Model Ts had been around for about 20 years, and they were considered the best, cheap, reliable automobile on the market, cheap being the operative word. Was it even possible for a machine to be more reliable than a horse or a mule? I seriously doubted it.

The larger machine was a four-door touring carriage with a hard top. The smaller two were both two-doors. One had a hard top and the other had a canvas roof. I asked how much he wanted for the touring carriage. Bottom line was, we settled on $450 for the four-door, provided he could teach me to drive first. The deal was struck.

He and I set to it. There was a lot of work involved just to start a machine. Just saying giddy-up and clicking your mouth wouldn't do it.

First step was to turn on the fuel shut-off valve, which is located under the hood on the right side of the engine.

Second, set the vertically mounted floorboard handbrake by pulling it all the way back, away from the dashboard to the seat. They called it a handbrake and it was, but it also served as the two forward gears (plus neutral) transmission shift lever. Pulling it all the way back into neutral prevented the vehicle from lurching forward as soon as you cranked it.

Third, make sure the ignition key in the dashboard is in the off position.

Fourth, adjust the spark advance all the way up to start the engine. It's located on the left side of the steering column. It allows the driver to set the timing on the engine so it runs smoothly.

Fifth, adjust the choke lever which is located on the front of the radiator, particularly if the engine is cold. FYI, there is also a choke knob on the dashboard. Pulling it out increases the flow of fuel.

Sixth, if the engine is cold, pump fuel into the carburetor by turning the crank four revolutions. It turns left to right. If the engine is hot, this is unnecessary. Note: This step is only done with the ignition key in the off position.

Seventh, now return to the dashboard and turn the ignition key on. That allows the internal battery to start the engine.

Eighth, set the throttle down below the middle to start the engine. It's the little lever on the right side of the steering column. Up reduces the flow of gas. Down increases the flow.

Ninth, crank the handle clockwise with your left hand, palm down, open fist, to start the engine. Never crank with your right hand. This is important in the event the engine backfires, which will slam the crank handle counterclockwise and can break your arm or thumb if your hand is closed. By using your left arm, a backfire will only jerk the crank out of your hand, not break your arm.

Tenth, once the engine starts, turn the ignition key to the off position to allow the magneto to generate the necessary electricity to run the automobile (thus saving the battery).

Eleventh, take your seat behind the steering wheel. Adjust the spark advance and throttle accordingly until the engine is running smoothly.

Twelfth, the Model T has three-foot pedals on the floorboard beneath the steering column. They're in a triangular V formation. Upper left is the clutch pedal. When the clutch is pushed in, you can shift into the two forward gears from neutral (which means not in any gear. It's an idling position). Upper right is the brake pedal. Push it in part way to slow down or all the way down to stop the vehicle. The lower middle pedal is the reverse gear pedal. With the engine running smoothly, to drive forward, depress the clutch pedal and put the transmission into gear by pushing the handbrake lever forward. Halfway is first (slow) gear and all the way forward is second (fast) gear. First gear allows the machine to accelerate up to 10 miles per hour. To obtain more speed, push down on the clutch again and push the handbrake lever all the way forward (into second gear). More speed means more fuel is needed. Push the throttle level up. (Push it down to reduce speed.) Top speed is now possible.

To slow down, push down on the right pedal (brake) with your right foot and ease off the throttle.

To come to a complete stop, find neutral by pushing the clutch in and moving the handbrake lever backwards. If you can't find neutral by feel, just pull the handbrake lever all the way back, and it will automatically go to neutral and set the handbrake. Also throttle down (by pushing up on the throttle lever) and continue pushing all the way down on the brake pedal.

To go into reverse gear, you must be at a complete stop. Push down on the clutch with the left foot and down on the reverse pedal with the right. To stop, let off the reverse pedal and push down on the brake pedal.

Learning to drive was a challenge. First, I had to get the infernal machine started. Then I had to master the two forward gears and the brake pedal. I learned that the machine was not really designed for going backwards, and to avoid doing so as much as possible.

The Model T had a 4-cylinder inline engine churning out 20 horsepower with a top speed of 42 miles per hour (as if anyone were that crazy). Also, the carburetor was gravity fed, so if you needed to drive up a steep incline, you had to drive up in reverse gear, understanding that the 10-gallon gasoline tank was stored under the front seat. It was the only way to get fuel to flow to the carburetor on a steep incline.

The Model T came with one spare tire on the back, but it wasn't mounted on a rim. Of course, tires have inner tubes, which need to be patched with glue before a puncture on the tire could be plugged. Anyone who ever owned a bicycle already knew how to fix a flat. The repair kit came with a jack, jack handle, tire punch, rubber plugs, rubber patches, small tube of glue, and bicycle pump. Mr. Grinstead demonstrated how to employ the jack. He said it took on average, two hours to change a flat tire. Ergo, it would be best to purchase another wheel and mount the spare tire on it already inflated. Then the punctured tire could be repaired at your leisure at home. After my first flat tire, I learned my lesson. I purchased a spare wheel.

Mr. Grinstead taught me to drive, so I consummated our deal. I paid him with four Benjamin Franklins and one President Grant. (When I went to the savings bank to withdraw the cash, I specifically asked for five $100s and two $50s with the rest in smaller denominations. Up until that day, I had never held a $50 bill in my hand, let alone a $100. I guess I was showing off a little bit.)

Since this pending purchase nearly cleaned me out, I decided to go ahead and close the account. At the end of the day, what was left of my savings went into a small metal lockbox hidden in my wooden Militia footlocker, which was secured with a padlock. I wore the key around my neck on a metal ball-chain. The footlocker was stashed under my bed. It's where I stored all of my treasures and important documents. Two years later on October 29, 1929, I was thankful I had closed out my account. That's when the stock market crashed and all the banks went belly up. Most folks lost everything. My folks lost some, but Chloe and I didn't lose a thin dime.

After Mr. Grinstead and I shook hands and agreed to be friends for life, I drove to the Jefferson County Courthouse. I paid 25 cents for my driver's license and $1 for the license plate. The property tax for the machine cost $2.75. Now I was street legal. Wasn't that easy compared with today?

Then I drove to Chloe's house and took her for a ride. I must say it was exhilarating. After I dropped her off, I drove home and took Mama out for a ride. She enjoyed it too, but she still fussed at me for spending my money foolishly. At the time, I thought she was probably right. When we got back, I cleaned out the old shed behind the house in the backyard so I had covered parking from the wintertime snow and ice. It wasn't much help from the occasional pigeon droppings. I quickly learned that keeping a black car shiny was an energetic endeavor.

Truth is, I didn't use the machine all that much. It became a real asset once the Great Depression set in, and especially during World War II. Then you couldn't buy motor vehicles, tires, guns, ammo, and many other things for love nor money. Tobacco, coffee, shoes, and sugar, among other common items were also scarce. Everything went to the war effort. If you didn't have it before January 1942, odds were you were SOL (shit out of luck). Fortunately, in addition to the automobile, I did have a fair stash of ammo. Sadly, I had none of the other items everyone craved so desperately.

Chloe and I married on September 17th, 1927. We spent

two nights in the Galt House to get better acquainted. Then it was time for both of us to go back to work. I promised her a real honeymoon during the fourth week of February next year so she could go to Mardi Gras in New Orleans. It fell on Tuesday the 21st. That truly energized her to save money. Overnight she metamorphosed from a Swede to a Scot. Ha!

We agreed that Chloe would continue to work until such time as she got heavy with child. For one thing, we needed the extra income. For another, Chloe needed to keep busy.

Where would we make our residence? We needed to find suitable lodging. It became a real conundrum. I thought I had resolved this before the wedding but it didn't work out. I had a place all lined up, deposit and all, but it caught fire the evening we wed. Fortunately we had not stored any of our belongings in it.

We went to my folks' house to see if we could spend a night or two. As a result of Mama's tears and Papa's reassuring words, we took up residence with them, at least for the time being. That was the initial agreement. Papa was still gone at least three days a week with his job, and Mama enjoyed our company. It seems that Chloe had bewitched both of them, just like she did me. Within a few weeks, our residence there became permanent. Mama maintained she couldn't get along without Chloe. Papa was happy too, so we settled in. I had already observed that it was fruitless to fight 'City Hall'. Besides, I was happy, too.

It worked out quite well, especially after Papa got down bad with the arthritis and had to retire. That was later on in 1936, when he was age 66 and had 44 years of service with the railroad. They gave him a nice gold pocket watch and attendant gold chain, plus a little pension, but it wasn't enough for a sparrow to live on. Social Security didn't become an entity until 1935, so it didn't come into play for either Papa or Mama, who never had a paying job. Even though they had squirreled away what they thought was a decent nest egg, they still needed some help. They were proud, and didn't want us to know. We did our best to pitch in without being obvious. All of this happened nearly a decade after we married. None of us saw it coming back in 1927. We were thrifty all, but still living high on the hog, at least from our frugal perspectives. Now we had to make some adjustments.

Something I never knew until after I wed, was that Papa bought the house back in 1905, with a mortgage he paid in full twenty years later. All I ever knew was he rented the house when they first emigrated from Scotland. So, Papa proposed, and we accepted, that Chloe and I pay no rent and they bought no groceries; further, he would pay the property taxes and electricity, and we would purchase the coal. It goes without saying that Chloe helped with the housework and cooking. I helped with the chores and by doing needed repairs. In addition, Papa had use of the Model T, and he drove it much more than I. Everything else sorted itself out.

In February of 1928, Chloe and I took the L&N train to Memphis. We switched to the train called the City of New Orleans, which took us the rest of the way to New Orleans. This was our belated honeymoon trip to Mardis Gras. We were gone a week. We lodged in the Hotel Monteleone on Royal Street in the Vieux Carré, otherwise known as the French Quarter. The Mistick Krewe of Comus held their ball there, and by a happenstance encounter with the King of the

Krewe, we were invited to attend as his guests. That was both a blessing and a curse, because Chloe needed to find a gown, and I needed to rent a tux. Nevertheless, this turned out to be the most memorable, upscale fandango we ever attended our whole lives. Chloe talked about it for years.

After three years on The Job, I got promoted to patrolman second grade. It came with a raise to $20 per week. I was still on a walking beat, but that was my choice. It was what I wanted. I personally knew all the business owners on my beat, and most of the residents. If they had a police matter, they brought it to me. I could never have had such an intimate relationship with the people I served had I been assigned a beat so large that it took a motorcar to cover it.

Chloe was making $9 a week at the apothecary. We were saving all we could for that rainy day which everyone hopes never comes. As I mentioned earlier, it went into our lockbox, not a savings bank which paid a paltry 1% in interest.

In March of 1929, Chloe told me she thought she was pregnant. In April, we knew for certain she was. She was just beginning to show in June. She quit work the end of the month. Her employer, the pharmacist Mr. Gibbons, was extremely sad to see her go. We were thrilled to be having a bairn, but our savings began to slow down like a train going uphill.

Then there was Tuesday, July 23, 1929.

It began like any other workday, except it was smoldering hot like the pit of Hades, and muggy like a Turkish steam bath. Just breathing was a perspiration-inducing endeavor. I was thankful we were no longer required to wear the wool tunic on such a day. Just touching the badge pinned to my chest burned my fingers. I was soaked through and through with sweat by the time I walked to work. So was everyone else. As such, we all expected a quiet day. It was too hot to fight or to steal, or so we reasoned.

Everyone was moving in slow motion. After roll call, I trudged back to my beat. For a while, I was able to walk on the shady side of the street. Then it was noon and the only shade to be found was under an awning or a full-grown tree, something fairly uncommon in the CBD. The thermometer on the clock tower said it was 97 degrees. Can you spell sweltering misery?

I made my fourth call of the day back to HQ from the callbox at the corner of 7th and Main. No messages for Beat 7. S.S. Kresge's Five and Dime was right there, so I decided to eat lunch. It had tall ceilings and lots of ceiling fans inside. It felt ten degrees cooler just as soon as I stepped inside and closed the wooden door. General Manager Cecil Cromwell was chatting with the front cashier clerk, Miss Rhonda Beasley. They both smiled.

Mr. Cromwell said, "Good to see you, Chet. Hot one today. Am I right?"

"Right as rain, which would be as welcome as finding a two-dollar bill in a Cracker Jacks box. Everything going well today?"

"Splendid. Anything I can do for you?"

"Nope. Thought I'd wash up and grab a bite to eat."

"Appreciate your business. Blue Plate Special is sauerkraut and wieners, biscuits and fresh butter, and apple cobbler. It's so hot today, we're serving iced tea instead of coffee unless you just gotta have it."

"Iced tea sounds wonderful. Tell the missus hello for me."

"Will do. Right back at you."

"Thanks."

I walked to the back of the store to the washroom and took care of business. My shirt looked like I had mopped the floor with it. I tidied up and walked back to the middle of the store, and bellied up to the middle of the three-sided lunch counter. By the time I took a stool, Carol Rae had stepped up to take my order. She asked, "What can I get you, Chet?"

"Think I'll take the Blue Plate Special."

"Iced tea or coffee?"

"Iced tea."

"Coming right up."

The meal was delicious. It was sufficient, but not overindulgent. Soon as I finished, Rhonda stepped over and said, "On the house today, Chet."

I replied, "Rhonda, you're as sweet as a basket full of baby kittens, but I can't take you up on it. I really do appreciate it, though. Mr. Cromwell needs to earn his living and so do you. Especially you. You got kids to feed."

The bill was 20 cents. I fished out a quarter and laid it on the counter. Then I stood up and stretched. I was dreading my return to the sweltering heat and attendant humidity.

Carol Rae smiled at me and scooped up the coin. She said, "Thanks. Chet, you're pretty sweet yourself. Have a nice day."

I threw her a salute and moseyed back down to the washroom. I needed to eliminate at least one of the glasses of tea, and wash up once more before hitting the bricks. My clothes were ringing wet with sweat and clinging to my body.

I could feel the sweat running down my leg into my sock. I briefly pondered becoming a nudist. Then I stepped out and began cruising down the aisle slowly towards the front of the store, like a century-old, sleep-deprived tortoise.

I was about 15 yards short of the door when I realized Rhonda was being stuck up by a pair of vicious scoundrels. I recognized the one nearer me, even though they were both wearing bandannas over their faces. His name was William C. Bayer. His moniker was Billy Bear. He was pointing a long-barreled, blue steel revolver at Rhonda. She had already given him the proceeds of the cash register in a paper bag, which he held in his left hand. He wanted what was inside the drop safe, which was cemented in a round hole in the floor behind the counter.

I had arrested Billy Bear twice in past years for general mopery. Once for stealing a bicycle and the other time for strong-arm robbery. He got jail time for both, not prison, but it obviously wasn't enough for him to cease his wicked ways. Now he had escalated to the Big Time. Armed robbery would net him 20 years at hard labor, assuming the judge was feeling compassionate and didn't sentence him to death or life. If he didn't hang, he'd soon be pounding big rocks into smaller ones.

I didn't recognize his beanpole partner, who stood closer to the door. He was waving a snub-nose blue steel revolver in the air like an energetic orchestra director. It was pointed in Rhonda's personal hemisphere. He kept saying over and over, "Come on, man. Let's go!"

I had drawn my revolver as I inched a little closer. Not too close. Distance was still my ally. They were so focused on

Rhonda, neither had noticed me. I picked my spot and stopped. I locked in my elbow, cocked, and aimed for Billy Bear's torso. I said softly, but firmly, "Drop the gun, Billy Bear. You too, Bones." They both jumped like goosed monkeys, pivoted, and trained their guns on me. Bones' eyes were as big as manhole covers. However, I was more focused on Billy Bear because he was closer to me and presented the greater threat.

Billy Bear wasted no time. He jerked off a round that blew a hole in a wooden box full of dolls which was on the shelving to my right. I responded in kind by putting two rounds in his chest before he could squeeze off a second shot. I could see the blood spray flying towards Bones. As Billy Bear crashed to the floor, Bones popped off four rapid fire shots at me. His first shot hit Billy Bear in his back. It was by accident I'm sure. The three other rounds made their way in my direction, but at the time I couldn't say where. Just the one which hit Billy Bear. I emptied my last four rounds rapid fire into Bones' torso. I was almost certain each one hit its mark. He had the most bewildered look on his mug before he collapsed to the floor.

I wasn't taking any chances. I dropped to my knees and ejected my empties. I reloaded from the spare cartridge slide on my belt. My reload drill was sloppy. I could feel the adrenaline coursing through my body in torrents. It was urging me to run. I had to clamp down hard and concentrate. I dropped two rounds and had to pick them up to complete the full reload.

Then I stood, pointed my revolver at Billy Bear's prostrate body, and walked over to where the two robbers lay. I carefully avoided stepping in the expanding pools of blood, which were leaking from the holes I had just pumped into their previously breathing, criminal bodies. I examined them closely. Both were already pushing up daisies.

Rhonda was sobbing and shrieking, hands over her face. I wasn't sure she even recognized me. Within seconds, the front of the store was filled with a dozen or so shoppers who tiptoed in from the rear. Two lifetimes later, Mr. Cromwell came running up from the back.

I asked him, "Could you call Headquarters and let them know I shot two robbers in your store? Ask them to send Sergeant Heim and the detectives. Tell them nobody else was hurt. Also, could you get a couple of clerks up here to watch the witnesses so they can be interviewed?"

He jumped right on it. There were 11 eyewitnesses, and only one had slipped away. Fortunately, one of the clerks knew her. It was Mrs. Rayburn, and he knew where she lived. In the meantime, I kept an eye on both robbers' guns and the sack of cash laying beside Billy Bear's body. At least it was out of the blood.

Somehow *Courier Journal* photographer Aaron LeCompte beat everyone to the store. Maybe he was just in the area and heard the shots. He snapped a photograph of the crime scene from the doorway while I was kneeled over Bones' body. I ran him off, but the damage was already done. Bet you can guess what was plastered on the front page of the newspaper the following morning.

First cops to arrive were Captain Nobles and Sergeant Heim. They were followed by Detective Lieutenant Onslow Gibbons and Detective Sean O'Toole. First, they checked to see if I were okay. I assured them I was. I gave them the rundown as to what happened. Captain Nobles chewed me out when I told him about Aaron LeCompte. They posted me on the outside of the front door to keep gawkers out. This was pending the arrival of Patrolman Lester Blackburn from Beat 10, the adjacent foot beat. Then they got down to work.

Patrolman Lester Blackburn came charging up, out of breath and about to faint from heat exhaustion. He may have been sent here to guard the front door, but he was out of commission. He spent the next hour recovering flat on his back on the cool tile floor of the men's washroom with a damp towel plastered on his forehead. I got him a large tumbler of water. Thankfully, he was okay.

Detective O'Toole took photographs and made measurements. Lieutenant Gibbons and Sergeant Heim interviewed witnesses and took statements. Captain Nobles supervised and made decisions. Eventually a hearse arrived and hauled the two stiffs to the morgue. It was close to 3 o'clock by the time they were done. We all went back to HQ except for Patrolman Blackburn, who was ordered to cover his beat and mine until shift change.

I learned that Bones was actually named Elton Gooch, 31 years of age. His monicker was Goober. He lived in a flophouse over on Becker Street on Beat 10. He was a small-time house burglar, not a stickup man. Our records revealed he had done one two-year stint in Eddyville for burglary of a house over on 22nd Street five years ago. He was carrying a .32 caliber, Iver Johnson 'Owl Head' revolver that they were pretty sure had been stolen a week ago in a house burglary on Constance Street. They'd know for sure tomorrow. Billy Bear was packing a .32 caliber, Harrington & Richardson revolver. So far as they knew, it was not stolen.

Both Captain Nobles and Sergeant Heim commended me for my quick response and action under fire. Captain Nobles even placed a commendation letter in my file. It was my first one for valor. They told me I could go home as soon as I wrote my report and turned it in to Lieutenant Gibbons. Sergeant Heim said he wanted to proof it first. Then they excused me so I could go upstairs to the Detective Bureau to write the report. It was factual but brief. I brought it down for Sergeant Heim to approve. He read it and smiled. He handed it back, and I took it upstairs. I was done before 5 o'clock. Then I walked home.

This was the first time I was ever shot at, and the first time I shot someone. It took me a few days to wrap my arms around it. After that, I doubled down practicing with my revolver, this time to include reload drills. The sloppy reload was something I never told anyone.

-5-
Looking Back

Looking back, I was a child until I married. Naive. I came up in a loving family. I enjoyed school. I was living my dream as a policeman. I went through the same ups and downs that most folks experience, but the bad times didn't last. I was happy, content, unworldly. My universe didn't extend much beyond the city limits and I didn't care. I wasn't curious. I had everything I needed, or so I thought.

By the grace of Providence, I met Chloe. She filled a void I didn't know existed. Hand-in-hand with her, I experienced joy beyond anything I could imagine. The Job was fun and gratifying and I loved it, but it paled in comparison with the time Chloe and I spent together. I did all I could to please her, and she returned it to me tenfold. Everyday was Christmas. I became a better person because of her. We didn't have an excess of money, but we had everything we needed. We had each other and that's all that mattered.

I had yet to experience the death of a loved one. None of us had suffered significantly regarding a health issue. I never thought about death, or old age, infirmity, or loss of a loved one. I had the eternal optimism of youth, and never imagined myself beyond age 30 or 35. I didn't notice that Time was quietly slipping through the hourglass. These were all fabulous years in Never Never Land, and I was Peter Pan.

Our son, Arnold Victor Sinclair was born on Tuesday, October 29, 1929. He was our pride and joy. Both his grandmas made over him. We were truly blessed. Papa bought him a toy train engine, which he wouldn't be old enough to play with for a couple of years. It wasn't lost on me. Papa was trying to turn Arnie into a railroad man. I couldn't blame him. Being a railroad man was my second career choice.

Unfortunately, Arnie's birth coincided with the Great Stock Market Crash, sometimes referred to as Black Tuesday. We didn't own any stock, so at first it didn't register. Then it did. It altered everyone's life throughout the world.

The Roaring Twenties roared past in a flash, leaving everyone behind in a crumbling world, dazed and confused. If you didn't know Jesus, you better make haste and find Him, because Satan was making a big play to steal everyone's soul.

Banks closed and depositors lost everything. The Federal Deposit Insurance Corporation (FDIC) didn't exist then. Businesses shut down. Folks lost their jobs. Anyone who still had a job clung to it for dear life, even if his wages were reduced or his boss was an ogre.

Other than churches, there were very few social welfare agencies. We began to see soup lines pop up. They helped, but it wasn't anywhere near enough. People were broke and hungry.

Suddenly, there were homeless bums everywhere, scrounging for anything worth expropriating when they thought no one was looking. It was called stealing, but most of the bums were harmless and just trying to survive. They had nowhere to go. Nowhere to turn. No one was hiring. Times were hard for everyone, especially for the destitute. They called these years The Great Depression. There wasn't anything great about it.

Some places there were riots, like in the Nation's Capitol. Great War veterans were issued Bonus Certificates in 1924 for services rendered during the war, but which did not mature until 1945. The veterans were destitute and needed the money now. They marched on Washington D.C., demanding relief. They referred to themselves as the Bonus Expeditionary Force (BEF), in a reference to the Allied Expeditionary Force (AEF), which defeated the Axis Powers in the brutal war. Some folks referred to these protestors as the Bonus Army. Only a decade or so earlier, we called these former American doughboys heroes.

All they wanted was immediate payment of what was due them because, as a result of the Depression, they were now out of work and their families were starving. Nothing more. They set up a shanty town, as neat and orderly and sanitary as the camps they had lived in during the war. It became their living quarters while they protested.

President Herbert Hoover lost patience with them. He sent General Douglas MacArthur and the U.S. Army to crush them with cavalry and tanks. MacArthur did his job exceedingly well from a military perspective, but it didn't set well with the American public. It cost Hoover his reelection, ushering in Franklin Delano Roosevelt as President. Eventually, the Government did make the bonus payments, but not when it was needed most.

Shanty towns like this one, minus the hygiene and civil protestors, sprang up like weeds near the railroad tracks in nearly all the bigger cities. They were dangerous places to be, especially for the young and the weak. Ever so often at the behest of City Hall, the Louisville Police Department teamed up with the L&N railroad dicks to send the shantytowners down the line. City Hall preferred displacement to anywhere away from our community, versus arresting them for any of a multitude of violations. Arrests meant housing them in jail. Then the taxpayers had to feed them, and they were too many.

Fights were always breaking out in shantytowns. Bums turned up dead. Absent the cops, shantytowns were ruled by jungle law. Survival of the fittest. Some folks died from disease brought on by cold and malnutrition. Others died at the hands of the predators in their midst. Ever now and then, one or two died at the hands of the railroad dicks or the police. The ones I witnessed die during the raids brought it on themselves; however, I'm certain there were other incidents in which they didn't.

We residents of 718 South Floyd Street were more fortunate than most. There were two wage-earners in the household. That being said, the railroads had less business, so Papa made fewer runs, so he brought home less income. Also, I was frozen in my pay status as a patrolman second grade for six years instead of four, when I was due a promotion to first grade. That's because there were no raises, no promotions, no new hires. The City was struggling to get by with less revenue coming in from taxes, after many years of prosperity which we all remembered fondly. I didn't dare squawk. I was fortunate to still have a job. Besides, once the economy recovered, the City made good on it.

One way the public could see that the City was broke, is they didn't have money to replace worn out uniforms. We patched up our old ones. Besides, they weren't hiring anyone, even if someone retired, quit, died, or got fired. Another indicator was some of the motor beats reverted back to foot patrols. I can tell you the patrolmen who got accustomed to driving instead of walking were some unhappy. Nevertheless, they kept their lips buttoned up. Don't like it? Quit then. That was the answer.

In addition, it hadn't been Jefferson County's policy to put inmates on road gangs, but we did in those days. Inmates classified as non-violent offenders became a heavily guarded adjunct to the City Works Department, which had lost a host of personnel due to cutbacks. The inmates cleaned up the debris left behind when we closed down the shantytowns. Otherwise, they cleaned up the streets and alleyways. The deputies guarding them were armed with shotguns loaded with buckshot. They had ironclad orders to shoot anyone who tried to escape. I can only recall an inmate trying it one time. He paid the ultimate price. That's all it took.

The road gangs got fed more rations than the inmates who stayed in lockup, so it wasn't all bad. They had many volunteers. The rations never had been great, but they were even worse during the Depression. Bowl of grits and one cup of coffee for breakfast. Two bologna sandwiches and a glass of tea for lunch. Large bowl of bean soup, slab of cornbread, and cup of coffee for supper, seven days a week. During the growing season, trusties worked a county-owned, ten-acre farm. All the produce they harvested went into the inmate menu. This included apples from a half-acre orchard. Also, if an inmate had someone on the outside who could afford it, they were allowed to bring a care package consisting of food items only, to the inmate on visiting day, which was once a week on Tuesday. That was it.

It goes without saying that I made more arrests during those years than before. Hard times foster a growth in all types of crime, but more so for economic crimes. Most of my arrests were for vagrancy, petty theft, trespassing, indecent exposure (which usually meant urinating or defecating in public), public drunkenness, disorderly conduct, vandalism, carrying a concealed deadly weapon, possession of burglary tools, and such. Most of the felonies I encountered were for grand larceny, burglary, assault, robbery, and the occasional murder or manslaughter. Regarding misdemeanors, I would usually give a guy who was passive and down on his luck a break once. Second time around I had no mercy.

In spite of the Depression, we still managed to have some good times. Franklin D. Roosevelt was elected President. His fireside chats on the radio perked folks up. Everyone could tell he was working around the clock to make things better. Things seemed to start picking up by 1934. Even so, that was after more than four years of deprivation and suffering. He created the Works Progress Administration (WPA) to employ people to carry out public works projects. He also created the Civilian Conservation Corps (CCC) to employ young, unmarried men to take on conservation projects in rural areas. Both agencies were temporary fixes to put unemployed people back to work until the economy turned around.

A monumental event occurred in 1933, when Prohibition was finally repealed. This was especially true in the Commonwealth of Kentucky, where more than 95% of all bourbon was distilled, aged, and from whence it was distributed throughout the nation and even to foreign nations. On the one hand, the main thing Repeal did was to make alcoholic beverages legal again. There never had been a shortage of alcohol during the Depression - just a shortage of legal alcohol. Therefore, Repeal's greatest accomplishment was to put legal distillers and their employees back to work, reduce the number of illegal distillers, and give local, state, and Federal governments a tremendous boost in tax revenues.

I think this pretty much covers most of my thoughts about the Great Depression, other than to say we survived it intact.

Arabella Elspet Sinclair was born August 16, 1933, during The Great Depression. She was a beautiful blond-haired, blue-eyed baby. As it turned out, she was to be our last child. She was quickly spoiled by both her grandmas. Mama's house was once again filled with the crying and cooing of a bairn. She already had the patter of little feet with Arnie.

Taking a short break for now. Will pick up from here in a little bit. Need to check my surroundings.

-6-
What's This All About?

At the beginning, I said someone is trying to kill me and I didn't know why.

Let me fast forward. Today is Friday, April 6,1973. My dear wife Chloe passed away two years ago at age 64. She died of a brain aneurysm. Neither she nor I saw it coming. The good news is she went fast. The bad news is I'm having a hard time getting over it. She was my everything. Honestly, I'm still a lost ball in the high weeds without her.

Backing up some more, I retired as a patrol sergeant from The Job ten years ago with 38 years of service. They gave me full credit for the time I spent in the Army. Like the monkey who was having sexual intercourse with the skunk said, "I haven't had all I want, but I've had all I can stand". I'd done enough and I was ready to go. We had an amicable parting. No sour grapes. I'm very pleased with my pension. No complaints there.

Chloe was a stay-at-home housewife and mom after she got pregnant with Arnie. Her hobbies included knitting, needlepoint, playing the piano, tending to her flower garden, reading, going to movies, baking, and of course looking after her family. My hobbies were watching baseball - the Cincinnati Reds are my team - shooting, tinkering on my automobile, fixing things around the house if I have the know-how. Otherwise, I call a professional. I like to fish a little bit, but I'm no bass fisherman with a fancy boat. I'm perfectly happy to bank fish with a cane pole like I did as a youngster. That's about it.

We both attended church regularly all our lives. Chloe was more active than I. I was plenty satisfied with just attending the church services. Not much of a social butterfly in church, nor did I volunteer for any church committees. Too much handwringing, posturing, and drama. We tithed, and I still do, but it's nobody's business but ours.

I retired in March, 38 years to the day I was hired. By autumn I was pretty bored. Not only that, truth is, Chloe got tired of me being under foot so much. She suggested I look for a part-time job. I concurred wholeheartedly.

I called an old retired cop buddy named Roscoe P. Walton. He had managed to wrangle the security contract for the new Kentucky State Fairgrounds, located in Louisville. He set up his security company from scratch, and initially hired about a dozen security guards - he calls them security officers - for full-time coverage. Everyone had to go through the process to get fully licensed as armed merchant police officers with arrest authority on the site they are hired to protect - nowhere else. It wasn't all that difficult. Take a few classes, pass the background check and the written examination. The license has to be renewed every four years. No biggie.

Roscoe provides the uniforms, which consist of dark blue trousers and light blue shirts similar to the police department's, except we don't have blue stripes on the trousers. We do wear a black tie. He also provides a dark blue, pullover sweater, and a short-waisted jacket similar to the Army's 'Ike Jacket' for cooler weather. Our caps are similar to the police department's, except the crown is six-sided blue fabric instead of circular. The shirts and the jacket have a circular shoulder patch on the left sleeve. It's blue with a yellow border and writing. It reads *Kentucky Merchant Police Company* inside the border and *Licensed* across the middle. The hat shield and badge are both made of nickel, so they have a bright sheen. The hat shield is a circle, just like the patch. The badge is in the traditional shield configuration like the police department's. It reads, *Kentucky Merchant Police Officer* and it includes your number. My number is 13. Go figure.

Truth is, merchant police officers seldom make an arrest, and if they do, they are nearly all misdemeanor arrests. They have to call the local police department to come and haul the arrestee off to jail. The merchant police officer must go to court and testify just like any regular police officer would. The problem is, each of these arrests exposes the merchant policeman and merchant police company to civil liability. They have no backup by the police department or Commonwealth Attorney's Office (District Attorney) if the arrestee files a civil lawsuit. Ergo, Roscoe had to obtain professional liability insurance in the amount of $100,000 for each officer, and $1,000,000 for the company. It ain't cheap, and that's why he only hires solid, retired cops.

Roscoe has his office in the main building of the Fairgrounds. He's there on weekdays during the day shift. He's also there almost all day and night during peak events, such as the Kentucky State Fair.

Since I hired on, the Kentucky Merchant Police Company has only owned one motor vehicle at a time. Right now it's a white, 1969 Plymouth Fury, two-door sedan, which Roscoe usually drives. For example, if one of us needs a vehicle to patrol the perimeter, we usually drive our own, and he reimburses us for mileage. Roscoe absolutely hates to loan out his company car, but he did eventually purchase four electric golf carts, and they really come in handy.

It's a good gig. The wages are fair, with overtime at 1-1/2 times the hourly wage for anything over 40 hours per week. Being the newbie, he started me on the midnight shift, which actually suited me just fine. Usually it was just one other guy and me, each manning a station halfway across the complex from one another.

The fairgrounds put up industrial clocks, each with a keyhole, scattered in 30 different locations. On the half-hour, we alternate making the rounds with an 8-inch round gadget which is secured in a brown leather pouch with a shoulder strap. It weighs about three pounds. It has a thin, round, calibrated cardboard insert inside the mechanism. It also has a key attached by a chain. We stop by each clock station, insert the key, twist it, and the gadget stamps the time and clock location number. Normally I make the rounds beginning on the half-hour, and the other guard makes them beginning on the hour, accounting for 16 rounds across our massive domain during an eight-hour shift.

At the end of the shift, we return the gadget to Roscoe or his lieutenant, Lawrence V. Oglesby. He retrieves the cardboard disk which records the times we key each clock. He puts the used disk in his files, and replaces it with a new one for the next night shift. The guys on the other shifts have plenty of activity, so it isn't necessary for them punch the perimeter clocks.

With these gadgets, the Fairgrounds management and

Roscoe can confirm that we checked the entire premises each night every half-hour. Between rounds, which take about 25 minutes, we have 'ass time'. We each have a padded chair on rollers and a small table inside the building with an internal phone. We can read, work crossword puzzles, or color pictures with crayons until it's time to make the next round.

I walk about five miles each night, so I stay in pretty good shape, especially for an old duffer. Once I got used to it, I liked working the midnight shift. I have very few people to deal with. It's quiet and peaceful. Chloe would pack me a light lunch which I ate about 4 o'clock. I usually bring a thermos of coffee and the newspaper, but sometimes I take a paperback book. I usually slept after I got off work, so I could have the evening and supper with Chloe.

This was the pattern until Chloe died. Then I began packing my own lunch and suffered through very lonely evenings. I hired a maid named Mrs. Thornton to clean the house and wash clothes once a week on Wednesdays. I usually eat my supper at a local diner named Margo's, and jawbone with the regulars until they close at 10 o'clock. Usually, if it's a work night, I go in early and visit with the shift supervisor until it's time to take up my post.

So . . . . a little over a month ago, in the wee hours of Thursday, February 22nd, George Washington's 241st birthday, may he rest in peace, I was making my rounds in the main building. Exhibitors had spent the day before setting up in both the large exhibit halls for the Southern Tractor & Farm Implements Trade Show. I thought the exhibits were fascinating, so I spent my time browsing between rounds. You have to make them in the same order each night, so I usually had to backtrack to start.

I had completed the East Hall and had just begun the West, when I saw movement out of the corner of my eye towards the back. It was about 4:45. The halls have subdued lighting at night, not nearly so bright as they would if the public were present, but not dark either. It startled me, so I crouched down just a little and began moving as quietly as possible in that direction. I was very glad that I wear soft-soled brogans to work.

Then I heard a noise in that same area, as if a table had been bumped, so I drew my revolver. I practically tiptoed to be even quieter. I didn't want to give away my position in the event this was a thief or saboteur. You know, perhaps a competitor trying to make trouble for his competition. I had just rounded a corner where the combines were parked, when this white guy, average height, wearing a black toboggan, brown, heavy work coat, blue jeans, and a blue bandanna over his face, popped up around the corner and fired one shot at me with a revolver.

I ducked down, and he retreated back around the corner. Then I kicked it into high gear, but I didn't announce myself. What was the point? He knew I was security. I was in uniform. By then I could see him running for the nearest exit. He hit the exit bar at full speed, knocking the door wide open. At this time I yelled, "Halt". Wasted my breath. Would I have stopped if the tables were reversed? Of course not!

I caught up as fast as I could and stepped outside. Even though we have tall light poles in the parking lot making nighttime bright, I couldn't tell which way he went. We were on asphalt and it was dry as a bone, so I never did pick up his trail. After ten minutes or so, I gave up and completed my rounds. Before I did, I ran into Barry Morris, the other night shift guard. He heard the shot and came looking for me. We searched the area high and low where I had been standing when the perp shot at me, but we found nary a thing. Nothing seemed to be damaged. No idea where the spent round wound up.

We returned to our posts and finished the night. That morning I told Roscoe what happened. I completed a company incident report with every detail I could think of. He asked if I wanted to report it to the police. I asked, "What's the point? What could they do? If it turns out to be anything, we have it all documented right here on the company report." He agreed. At the time, we all assumed this was not directed at me, per se. Just a thief or commercial saboteur trying to make his escape from an alert security officer.

Three weeks later on Friday, March 16th, I stopped by the A&P (Atlantic & Pacific Tea Company - a national chain grocery) located at the corner of Hill and 6th Streets after I got off from work. I was still wearing my uniform. It was about 8:30. I was out of country ham, which I eat by the carload. It's my favorite meat. I also needed some more frozen orange juice and a few other things, like frankfurters and buns. Thankfully, I wasn't picking up anything with a glass container.

I was parked nose in on the side of the building in the very first space. There weren't many customers yet. I went in and made my purchases and returned to my car. I only had one paper sack of groceries, which I was holding in my left arm while I fished out my car keys from my right jacket pocket.

Somehow my key ring got snagged on a thread in my pocket, so I set the bag down on the ground so I could cut it with my pocketknife. I had just bent over when a shot rang out. It went whizzing right over my stooped body and hit the brick wall of the grocery in front of me, shattering pieces of brick everywhere. Naturally, I drew my revolver as I scurried in front of my automobile for cover, kicking over my sack of groceries and ripping the sack.

The shot came from behind me somewhere down the street, possibly from a dark-colored Ford Galaxie which was just turning South on Poindexter at a high rate of speed, tires squealing. Poindexter was about 150 yards from where I had parked. There weren't that many folks out and about, so the shot went completely unnoticed so far as I could tell.

I dusted myself off and checked the brick wall in front of my automobile. A two-inch divot was in the wall roughly 5-feet, 6-inches high. I searched until I found the slug. It was a copper-jacked, .30 caliber bullet with the nose all smashed in and mushroomed out. It looked to me like a .30-30 or a .30-06. You could make out the rifling on the rear, lateral portion of the projectile. I put it in my pocket, hoping someday I would find the would-be assassin's rifle to compare it with.

The first shooting was now looking more like I was the pre-selected target and not just a snoopy security officer. I probably should have reported both of these shootings to the police, but other than the slug I just salvaged, I had no evidence, no witnesses, no suspects. I didn't have anything to hide personally, but I still didn't want the police to focus on me, as in, "What did you do to piss somebody off bad enough to try to shoot you twice? Why don't we turn your life upside down to see what you did wrong? It must be something."

True. It must be something. It still doesn't mean I want the police dissecting my life to determine if I was the initial aggressor who deserved a comeuppance. Somebody's gotta be at fault, so why not blame the victim?

I did tell Roscoe when I saw him Monday morning. I wrote another company incident report just to preserve the facts. I also taped the spent projectile to a 3-by-5-inch index card, dated and signed, enclosed in an envelope, and stapled to the incident report which Roscoe filed.

That's also when I began going through my scores of numbered and dated police notebooks, searching for some righteous gangster(s) I had put away who finally got out of the joint and decided to get even. I started with the very first notebook dating back to 1925, just to be thorough. It brought memories rushing back from my very first day on The Job when I learned how to memorize faces from mugshots.

I kept thinking about how the first shooter got into the building. The doors were all locked at quitting time. You could exit by pushing the breaker bar, but you couldn't get in without a key unless someone from the inside let you in. Originally, I thought he had secreted himself somewhere before all the vendors left for the evening. I still believe that, but why wait until 4 in the morning to take me out? It didn't make sense.

Then I thought about the A&P incident. It would suggest the shooter(s) followed me from work. I was still in uniform and my vehicle is easily identified. In 1950, I finally sold the Model T Ford for a two-tone, dark-blue-over-medium-blue, 1950 Studebaker Champion Regal Deluxe, two-door sedan.

This is the model in which the front end resembles a rocket ship. They refer to it as a bullet nose. The colors alone are striking. The car is an antique, and the styling is unique. Once someone sees it, he will never forget it, whether he likes it or not. Me, I lusted for that machine when I first laid eyes on it. I cheerfully paid the full asking price of $2,287.

The bottom line is, I am easy to follow and to identify. Whoever shot at me missed twice. They say the third time's a charm. What was I going to do about it?

Forewarned is forearmed. I had to presume the perp(s) also knew where I lived.

As soon as I returned home, I checked my property for any evidence of a prowler. I saw nothing. Then I asked my nearest neighbors if they'd seen anyone lurking around, or if a stranger had asked about me. The answers were no.

I examined my house carefully from the perspective of an intruder. I had done this numerous times before and the results were always the same. A determined intruder would have no difficulty gaining access, even though the windows and doors were locked.

The house is a single-story, wooden clapboard dwelling, painted white. The front and back doors plus the trim are painted a forest green. It was originally built in 1892. It was brand new when Papa first leased it. The landlord built it to be a rent house to bring in some revenue in his declining years. It's had many modifications since then, to include indoor plumbing (one bathroom), back porch kitchen fully enclosed, electric lights and fixtures, natural gas furnace, worn pine floors upgraded to oak, and ceiling fans in each room, just to name the major home improvements. There is no air conditioning.

It's 1,364 square feet with three bedrooms, a front parlor, eat-in kitchen, and a tiny den in the back. Each room has at least one wooden-framed window with screens. In hot weather, we slide the windows up. They latch from the inside, but breaking one of the window panes to reach in and turn the latch would be child's play. Ditto for kicking in either the front or back doors.

The front porch is covered as is the patio in the back. The shed in the backyard has been fully converted into a garage with a concrete floor and electric lights. Two parallel, 18-inch wide concrete strips serve as the driveway going out to the street. The backyard is clearly defined by wire, farm-style fencing. It's mostly there to add definition to the boundary. It wouldn't keep a 10-year-old kid out. The doors in the front of the garage open like batwings. I have a hasp and a padlock on it, but any determined thief would make quick work of that. Mostly the lock is there to hold the doors shut. None of these features were ever truly designed for the purposes of security. In the 69 years I've lived here, we've never had a burglary. As a youth, our protection from an intruder while we were home was in the form of my papa and his single-shot, Sears & Roebuck, 12-gauge shotgun loaded with double-aught buckshot.

We have a cellar, for which the only access is from the outside, via a horizontal, heavy corrugated metal door on a concrete foundation. It's secured by a heavy grade hasp and padlock. This is where we shelter during heavy storms such as tornadoes. Pull the door up to open, and descend down the concrete steps. There's a single naked light on the ceiling with a string pull to turn it on or off. The door can be locked from inside by a heavy crossbar. This is our best place to shelter in terms of security. However, the cellar was dug after the house was built, so it has no access into the house itself. Nevertheless, it's the safest place on the premises for persons to shelter or to secure valuables, of which I have very few.

Nearly everything we've ever owned could be replaced by insurance. The most precious items have always been pictures or family keepsakes which, for the most part would be of no value to a thief. Once Chloe passed away, I gave everything of value she owned to Arabella.

The one item I kept was her gold wedding band. It's in an old cigar box I use for small keepsakes. It's in a vertical wooden cabinet in the cellar, along with Papa's shotgun and my .30-06, Model 1903 Springfield rifle I bought from the Civilian Marksmanship Program (CMP) when I returned from World War II. I wanted an M-1 Garand like I carried in the war, but they hadn't released them yet for sale to the public. That's also where I keep my gun cleaning kits and stockpiled ammo. I have nearly a full box of buckshot (in waxed paper shell casings left over from Papa), 210 rounds of .30-06, and 12 boxes of .38s. I keep a partial box of .38s in my bedside nightstand. For these reasons, I've never been afraid of a burglary. I've always been more concerned about fire, which would consume everything inside the house.

I do have two burglar alarms in the form of a 7-year-old fixed yellow tomcat named Bixby, and a spayed 4-year-old female rat terrier named Dink. Bixby belonged to Chloe and Dink belongs to me. She's mostly white with a few black spots, a little splash of black on the top of her head and ears, and a brown patch on one side of her face. Bixby alerts if he hears a noise, but he doesn't meow. Dink sets up a ruckus if someone she doesn't know comes around. That's it besides me with my .38 caliber revolver.

After my review, I decided not to make any changes. I refuse to live in fear. If I find out who tried to kill me, I'll take the battle to him/them. If I don't and he decides to let up, I guess I'll never know. I can live with that, too.

With this explanation of my current situation I will return to my narrative where I left off.

-7-
Life in My Middle Years

I'll begin with both of my kids. Both Arnie and Arabella were healthy, happy kids. They both excelled in school. They walked or rode the city bus to the same schools we did at their ages. These were happy, fulfilling years. Arnie played baseball from the moment he was big enough to swing a bat. He lettered twice in high school and again in college. He graduated from Male in 1947, and the University of Louisville in 1951, with a Bachelor's Degree in Economics. Upon graduation, he enlisted in the Army. He didn't have a lot of choice. With the Korean War going on, he would have been drafted anyway. That being said, he was anxious to serve. After Basic Combat Training (BCT), they sent him to Officer Candidate School (OCS).

2nd Lieutenant Arnold V. Sinclair, Company A, 17th Infantry Regiment, 7th Infantry Division, was killed in sction the night of July 6, 1953, in the second Battle of Pork Chop Hill. Prior to the battle, he had been awarded the Combat Infantryman's Badge, Bronze Star with "V" Device, Army Commendation Medal, National Defense Service Medal, Korean Service Medal, and the United Nations Korean Service Medal. He was awarded the Purple Heart posthumously. Interment was at the Zachary Taylor National Cemetery in Louisville. He left behind his grieving parents and sister, and none of us have ever recovered. I still think about him nearly everyday. I miss him with all my heart. I pray he and Chloe are reunited in Heaven.

Arabella graduated from the last class of Louisville Female High School in 1950, before it became co-educational and renamed DuPont Manuel High School. She graduated from Louisville Baptist Hospital's Nursing Program in 1953, with a Registered Nurse's diploma and an occupational license. In 1956, she married Randolph Abernathy Lee, M.D. They relocated to Richmond, Kentucky, where he set up a practice as a family physician and she became his office nurse. They have two children, Fiona Heather Lee, born in 1960, and Barclay Calan Lee, born in 1964. I never get to see them often enough, but suffice it to say, they all seem fulfilled and very happy.

Perusing my police notebooks, I only found a half-dozen potential suspects. Other possibles had already passed away so far as I could ascertain. This is the hit parade I compiled prior to World War II.

In 1935, I arrested an 18-year-old thug named Delbert S. Finnegan. It was day shift and I was making my rounds in the CBD. Just before entering Cox's Liquors, I looked through the window and saw he was robbing the merchant, Jacob Steiner, with a revolver. I stood to the side of the building out of view and waited for him to exit. When he did, pointing my revolver directly at his chest from six feet away, I yelled, "Halt. Police!" He spun, aiming his gun at me, and I drilled him once. He went down like a two-ton elephant just fell on him from high in the sky. I thought he was a dead duck, but somehow he managed to survive. I missed an artery. He got life in Eddyville. I thought that was the last I'd ever see of him. Maybe not. I called the prison and they told me he was released in 1965. They had no address for him. No next of kin. He'd be 56 now. That would be a long time to hold a grudge. Besides, he's had eight years to look me up. I classify him as a possible, not a probable.

In 1938, I was partnered up with Patrolman Russell D. Roach. We called him Stick because he was tall and lean like a vertical human version of the insect known as a walking stick. He was three years junior to me. He was driving, and I was riding shotgun in a new, marked, 1938 Dodge coupe. By then we had been blessed with police radios in our units for nearly six years. That, plus the modern, less temperamental, and easier to operate vehicles, made a motorized patrolman's job infinitely better than our earlier years in Model T Fords without radios.

The call boxes were still part of the police landscape and got hourly usage from the walking beats, but access to a radio made response time so much quicker. On this particular day, Stick and I were assigned Beat 4, which covers the South End including Southern Parkway and Iroquois Park. We didn't need a call box.

We received a radio call about 1 o'clock from Headquarters regarding two suspicious characters (only description was white males) loitering near the Kentucky Trust Bank on Taylor Boulevard. The anonymous caller stated the subjects arrived about 20 minutes prior in a late model, gray Chevrolet sedan. The caller thought the way they were acting, they were up to no good.

Stick got on the stick and away we went, sans red light and siren. Didn't need them yet. This was a Code 1 call. When we got close, Stick slowed way down. We approached the bank from the side on Hazelwood Avenue. We stopped and scanned the area in the vicinity of the bank parking lot. We spotted a Chevy which matched the description. We eased up a little closer. No one was in the suspect vehicle, so we eased up even more. The windows were down and the engine was running. This had all the earmarks of a bank robbery in progress.

Stick parked. He called in our arrival and said we'd both be out on foot. He pointed to me that the key was still in the ignition. Then he turned off the engine. We both began to exit. Stick beat me out because I was retrieving the Great War, Army surplus, Winchester Model 12 Trench Gun. It's a 12-gauge pump shotgun with a 20-inch, open-choked barrel, meaning it's better for close range where the shot pattern is tighter. It holds six shells in the magazine plus one in the pipe. By the time I was ready, Stick was already 20 feet in front of me.

I hadn't anymore gotten out of the vehicle and disengaged the safety, when two masked mopes came barreling around the side of the bank in our direction. One was way out in front of the other. Guess they hadn't looked first before they turned the corner. Now they were both committed because they were in an alley. Both were wearing a red bandanna to conceal their faces. Both had a revolver in hand. One was also carrying a cotton bank bag full of what - free Tootsie Rolls passed out by the bank tellers to the children of depositors? Not!

Stick was much closer than I. The nearer bandit with the bag shot him before he uttered a word, although his service revolver was in his hand. Stick crumbled to the ground. I blasted the shooter in the torso which gutted him like a fish.

His gizzard and guts were flying every which way in a bright red mist. He collapsed to the ground and lay still.

The other bandit, who was farther away, continued to plow straight ahead towards me. He appeared to be undeterred from his partner's demise, but he did snap off a hasty shot at me in return for upsetting his applecart, I suppose. It was like he hadn't formulated a Plan B.

He was running hard and sucking wind. His shot was way off the mark, but it sealed his fate. I blasted him too, but the distance between us allowed the buckshot to spread out way too far, and only two of nine .33 caliber balls struck him - one in his left chest and one which passed through his left cheek and exited through the right, shattering a few teeth along the way. I chambered another shell, ready to finish him off.

This is what saved him. He shrieked like a constipated Comanche defecating hot coals, and let his gun fall to the ground. He jerked his hands up high in the air. He was wailing and moaning loudly in unfettered agony, but I had very little compassion. In fact, I had zero. My partner might be dying. I ran up and spun lucky boy around like a top, and cuffed him behind the back. Then I shoved him forcefully to the ground. I told him my next shot would be fatal if he even thought about getting up.

Then I scurried over to Stick. He was hit in the chest, but thankfully it missed his heart. He whispered, "I'm sorry."

To comfort him, I said, "Shush. Hold on, man. You're gonna be okay. Sit tight while I call for assistance. Be right back. Hang on."

I ran back to our unit and got on the horn. I keyed the mike and said, "Unit 4B. Need assistance, Code 3. Officer down.

Request an ambulance." Then I tore into the trunk of our car and found the first aid kit. All I needed was the gauze roll. I ran back and unbuttoned Stick's shirt. I made a thick pad out of the roll and placed it over his entry wound and pushed down as hard as I could to staunch the flow of blood.

I lost track of time, but it couldn't have been long. Screaming sirens and screeching tires and singularly-focused cops and gawking bystanders all showed up like we'd just discovered gold in a public swimming pool full of nudists. I do remember Patrolman Kirby L. Porter from Beat 3 was the first to arrive. He took over for me regarding Stick. I looked around and suddenly it seemed like everyone on the police force was there. I briefed Sergeant Heim and then got out of everyone's way. I went back and sat in the Dodge cruiser, my ride back to HQ. They rushed Stick to the hospital. Ditto for the wounded perp. Stick made a full recovery. So did the perp. I received my third citation for valor. It went into my file with the other two. The citations were appreciated. It meant I 'done good' and somebody important had noticed.

Lotta guys go all the way through their careers without getting a citation - not even for commendable and faithful service over a period of years. Something's wrong there. Was the officer a slug? Did the bosses hate him? What? Surely he did something commendable in all the years he was on the job.

Then I thought of Fatso Froggett. Maybe these officers really didn't deserve any commendations. Fatso was the type of employee who had to back up to the payroll clerk with his hand outstretched behind him to receive his paycheck. You know. Avoid eye contact because he never hit a lick at a snake and everyone knew it. An oxygen thief misidentified as a valued employee. A complete waste of mankind. Shameful.

Getting back on point, it turns out the bandits were 20-year-old identical twins - Lonnie Joseph Butts and Ronnie Joseph Butts. Ronnie was dead. He was the one who shot Stick. Lonnie lived. He went to prison for life. He got out of stir last year. No known address, but his next of kin was listed as his sister, Kimberly Tate, of 8844 New Cut Road. Lonnie was 55-years old. He was a strong possible.

Next up was Gordon T. Bertram from 1941. We were shorthanded on the midnight shift so that's where I was reassigned. At least I got Beat 4 on the South End, which is what I asked for. I was a one-man unit. Beat 4 was considered an average risk assignment, and since we were shorthanded, the only two-man units were on the high risk beats. I was fine with that. I'd much rather be alone than get paired up with someone I didn't gee-haw with very well.

Around 2:30, I received a prowler run on the west side of Southern Parkway in the 1800 block. The caller was anonymous. This was in a high rent district.

Southern Parkway has equestrian trails on both sides of the divided boulevard. Actually, each trail is as wide as a two-lane highway. They're unpaved with little round brown pebbles. Iroquois Park is at the southern terminus of Southern Parkway, and they have stables there to board or rent horses. This is a horse lover's paradise.

Prowler runs on midnight shift are fairly common, but seldom result in an arrest. This is because by the time we arrive, the prowlers usually have already slunk off. If the caller left a name and address, we'd check his property and the adjacent properties extra carefully. Afterwards we would meet him (but usually her) face-to-face, promising to check the area several times throughout the night. Prowler runs tend to be mostly PR runs to let the public know we are concerned for their safety.

One phenomenon I learned early on, is that there are a lot more insomniacs in the world than one might imagine. Most of them are lonely old widows who live alone, except for the cat. They all have a cat. These geriatric dears stare out their windows at night because they can't sleep. They see everything, too.

They know which neighbor is a drunk or cheating on his wife, or vice versa. Ditto for teenagers sneaking out of their bedrooms for a midnight rendezvous with their mischief-maker buddies or underage lovers. These are the bad boys who vandalize things.

Some callers leave their names and addresses with dispatch because they need to talk to an officer in the flesh. Find out his name. Who works this beat. Thank him personally for responding. Some even offer a cup of tea or a plateful of cookies if he will just stop and chat for a few minutes. Most cops do because they care. Loneliness is a long lane to navigate without many lights.

Other callers don't leave their names, but they will call Police Headquarters and complain if they didn't think the patrol unit spent enough time looking for the prowler.

In my experience, these were the most common types of prowler runs. I was a little jaded. It's what I anticipated that night. What I got was quite the opposite.

After the squeal, I crept northbound, slowly up the

parkway from Iroquois Park. I took my time, looking for suspicious person(s). Even though it was cold, I rolled both front windows all the way down so I could better hear faint sounds which could be significant. Nary a pedestrian nor a motorist were in sight, so I turned off my lights. Now I was a nearly inaudible, black shadow creeping slowly down the street like a predator hunting another predator.

To my surprise, I observed a subject in dark clothing jimmy open a window on the verandah of one of the brick bungalows. Then he climbed through the window, quiet as a stalking cat. I couldn't see the house number. The dwelling was dark, no lights inside, and no illuminated porch light. I had no idea if the occupants were home or not. Maybe the house was vacant because the owner was out of town or recently deceased. Maybe the residents were in bed fast asleep. It would be much worse all the way around if the owners were at home now that a burglar was inside. I was in the midst of another adrenaline rush. This was one reason I loved this job so much.

I kept on rolling in slow mo. I made damn sure not to step on the brake pedal which would illuminate my brake lights and give me away. I went another full block, made a U-B (U-turn), then parked on the horse trail. I called Dispatch, reporting that I was out of my unit on foot at the target location. Then I got my flashlight and locked up. I stepped off the gravel and trotted through the grass in the front yards to be quieter and to arrive on scene faster. I didn't know the street address of the house, but I knew I would recognize it.

All was clear when I arrived. It was too dark to see much of anything. I crept up to the house and onto the verandah.

The window was still open. It was ever so slight, but I could hear movement inside, so I concluded the burglar was still there. I decided to wait on the north end of the verandah, and ambush him as he made his exit, assuming he would come out the same way he went in. I didn't want to risk getting shot by the homeowner if he were home, nor did I want to precipitate a gunfight inside the house. God forbid!

Time passed like molasses in wintertime. I kept checking my watch. It was a Ball railroad watch, known for its accurate timekeeping. The time was 2:55. I'd been on scene eight minutes. It was all I could do, not to rush in, turn on the lights, and yell, "Halt! Police!"

At 3:04 I heard a noise. A white pillowcase stuffed to overflowing was carefully placed on the floor of the verandah in front of the open window. Seconds later, the intruder slipped out without a sound. He was crouched down with his back to me. It was pitch dark, but I could still make out his profile. I didn't wait for him to stand up. I didn't want him to stand. I wanted him off-balance. I uttered very softly, "Hands in the air, or you're a dead man. Flinch, and I'll shoot."

I reinforced my command by slowly cocking my revolver. I wanted him to hear that distinctive click, click, click of the rotating cylinder and the locking mechanism of the hammer in the absence of any other sounds in that eerie midnight darkness. He did not obey.

Instead, he stood erect suddenly, and spun around on me. All I could see was the motion of his shadow. I couldn't even begin to see the sights on my revolver. Nevertheless, I pulled the trigger and shot him one time right there where he stood. At least I thought I did, if just for a moment. I couldn't tell if he had a weapon, but he was a felon caught in the act. That's all the law required in those days. Besides that, his movement was aggressive, and we could barely make each other out in the darkness. I definitely wasn't going to wait around for him to plug me first.

I was convinced in my heart-of-hearts I hit him, even though all I actually saw was the muzzle flash of my gun for a split second. Nevertheless, he vaulted over the brick bannister and began scrambling south. I flicked on my flashlight with my left hand and ran down the steps. My revolver was still in my right hand. Now I could see his back clearly, and I could tell he was hit. He was limping, and starting to slow down.

"Stop right now or I'll shoot you again! I mean it!"

He slowed down and then he stopped. He dropped the loot he had stolen. I waited and waited. Finally, he raised his hands in the air. He was still facing away from me. I sensed his indecision. Was he armed? I ran up on him and holstered my weapon. I grabbed his left arm forcefully and snapped the first cuff on his wrist. Then I jerked his right arm back and repeated the process on his right wrist. Then I spun him around facing me and gave him a vigorous toss. I treated him roughly to reinforce that he was no longer in control.

Three things suddenly became crystal clear.

First, I shot him in his upper left thigh. It wasn't bleeding all that bad, so I missed his femoral artery. He would live.

Second, I recovered a snub-nose Smith & Wesson revolver in his right trouser pocket. He was armed and 'ready for Freddy'.

Third, I knew this asshole! His name was Gordon T.

Bertram. He was an ex-cop. The City fired him a year ago for possession of stolen property. He got caught wearing the engraved Bulova wristwatch he stole from a drunk driver he had arrested. The victim's case was ultimately dismissed, and Bertram was unceremoniously terminated. The Commonwealth Attorney let him plead guilty to grand larceny, for which he received three years on probation, meaning he was a convicted felon before tonight. He was a disgrace to all LPD police officers.

Suddenly, the front porch light flicked on in the yard in which we were standing. The homeowner, a Mr. John Johnson, stepped out in his night shirt and bare feet. He did have on his fedora. He asked, "Can I help, Officer?"

"Yes, Sir. I just caught this man breaking into your next-door neighbor's house. I shot him and he needs an ambulance. Could you call Police Headquarters and tell them what I just said, and ask them to send Sergeant Haskell Moore and a detective right away?"

"Sure thing. Just so you know, my neighbor, Ernest Potts, and his family are out of town. Ernie's father just died, and he lived in Bowling Green. If you want, I can try to call him at his dad's house. I have the number."

"Sir, that would be most appreciated."

"Sure thing. Be right back. Don't let that dung beetle bleed on my sidewalk! I'll make him lick it all off if he does. I'm serious!"

"You bet."

Bertram survived, of course. The DB (Detective Bureau) went right to work on him. The sackful of stuff he stole in the Potts' house was worth over $1,300. Detectives obtained a search warrant for Bertram's house. They found over $35,000 of stolen goods, all of which originated from 26 different burglaries in Louisville. Another $25,000-worth of property from these same 26 burglaries was never recovered. Some of the burglaries even occurred on Bertram's beat while he was at work! The DB was able to clear each of these burglaries as solved cases.

I had Bertram on felon in possession of a firearm and dwelling house breaking (called burglary in some states). The detectives had him on 26 counts of RSP (receiving stolen property) because they couldn't prove he actually committed the burglaries, but it didn't matter. RSP was a felony charge, too.

Judge Haywood T. Storm found him guilty of 28 separate felonies, plus probation violation. Because Bertram was an ex-cop, he was held to a higher standard than the average mutt. Not only that, he had already violated the public's trust, topped off by violating his probation. Therefore, to make an example of him, Judge Storm sentenced him to serve the maximum sentence of 138 years in prison, all sentences to run consecutively, known as 'stacking' in jailhouse parlance.

I called Eddyville and discovered he had been released on parole a year-and-a-half ago. He's 72 years old now. He resides in an apartment complex at 120 Saint Joseph Avenue in Shively, which is a small city adjacent to, and southwest of Louisville in Jefferson County.

I received my fourth citation for valor. I also was included in a separate citation honoring Detective Sergeant Haskell Moore, his partner, Detective Jack Cohen, and me for solving a high profile serial burglary case, recovering $35,000 in stolen property, and securing a conviction with a 138-year prison sentence levied on the perpetrator. That was a first for me! Very glad to receive it!

I definitely consider Gordon T. Bertram a very strong possible.

The Bertram case concluded on Tuesday, December 2, 1941.

Life changed for everyone in the entire world on December 7, 1941, when the Japanese bombed Pearl Harbor. I realize now that I've unintentionally reported several events out of sequence in this narrative, which may have made things a little confusing. World War II was the most monumental event which happened in my lifetime, so I want to put it down on paper before I finish my quest to identify the other person(s) who may be trying to kill me. I hope you understand.

-8-
Signing Up

As soon as the world heard about the bombing of Pearl Harbor, I knew I had to enlist. Arnie was 12 and Arabella was 8. We had some bucks stashed away, but not enough for my family to survive on for two years, which is how long I figured it would take. Wrong! I also knew the Army pay was dismal, especially for the lower enlisted ranks. Chloe knew me better than I knew myself, and although she didn't want me to go, she knew I would never respect myself if I didn't, so she gave me her blessing. Besides, there was always a sizable chance I'd get drafted anyway.

On December 12th, I broached the subject over supper with the entire family, including my folks. The kids were taken by surprise. Arabella burst out in tears. Thankfully, I had waited until after we had completed the meal including our pecan pie à la mode for dessert.

Just when I thought all was lost, Papa saved the day. He said, "Chester, I've been waiting for this, and frankly, I was surprised it took you this long. I had these very same feelings when the Spanish War broke out. I knew I had to go, and so did Grandma. Everything turned out just fine.

"Arabella, Sweetie, things will be okay. Your papa needs to do this because our whole nation is in peril. If strong men don't stand up, the Japanese and Germans will conquer the world and make us all slaves. Grandma and I are here, and we aren't going anywhere, and neither is your mama. I will protect you just like your papa does. We will win this war and then all our servicemen can return home to their families. Your papa is doing this because he loves us all. He loves America. He wants us to be safe. Do you understand?"

"Yes, but I'm still scared. I'll miss Papa when he is gone."

"We all will, Sweetie. That's why we will pray for him every evening when we sit down to supper. Besides, I know he will write to us every chance he gets. You and Arnie can take turns reading his letters out loud to all of us over supper. Deal?"

"Deal." Then she ran over and jumped into my lap and hugged me with every bit of strength she had.

On Monday the 15th, I went to sign up for the draft. I was 37 years old and the age limit was 38, so they considered me an old man. It definitely wasn't as easy as when Papa signed up. I left the house at 6:50 to get a head start, but when I arrived at the Louisville Armory, the line of volunteers was already two blocks long. The sneak attack by the Japanese a week ago had riled up and unified the populace more than anything I had ever experienced. I took my place at the end of the line and resigned myself to a long wait. It was 38 degrees with cloudy skies when I left the house. At least the wind wasn't blowing nor was it raining or snowing.

Since we were on a wartime footing, the War Department had consolidated the processing for both volunteers and draftees. Also, it didn't matter which branch a volunteer wanted to join. The processing for all was in one central location. Heck, even the Coast Guard, a branch within the U.S. Treasury Department, was processed here. That's because during wartime, the Coast Guard is placed under the Navy, just like the Marine Corps.

When I finally did get to the front of the line, I was surprised to learn the processing would take several days; however, the various screenings/examinations were numbered, so you could pick up by going to your next processing area on following days without waiting in line outside.

Phase I was filling out forms with all your biographical data. They wanted to know more about you than your mother did. They definitely wanted to know you were who you said you were, so they asked a whole lot of questions about who all you were related to and how. They wanted to see identification if you had it. Many did not. Some men never obtained a driver's license. Many were born at home and didn't have a birth certificate. This was one reason they took your fingerprints.

Anyway, I sailed through all that. I opened my leather satchel and showed them my birth certificate, plus my National Guard Honorable Discharge Certificate (NGB-22), Louisville Police Department identification card, and my Male High School diploma to help sway their decision my way. Truthfully, they didn't seem all that eager to select me. They were more concerned about my advanced age, if you can believe that. Actually, I was a little miffed.

Phase II consisted of two written tests. It included an IQ test and a general aptitude test which they called the GT, for general test. It was designed to see which things you were good at and which you weren't. They didn't want to put someone with low math skills in a math intensive occupation such as artillery or engineers.

They never tell you how you do on the IQ test, but they will tell you how you did on the GT. I was in the top 10%, so I was qualified to go any direction they wanted to send me. That was as far as I got on the first day. Come back tomorrow, so I did.

Phase III was broken up into subcomponents. The first of those was an overall physical examination. Get naked in a large room with a dozen other naked men and let them inspect you. It's like you're a thoroughbred up for auction. They check everything, including all your orifices. They even check between your toes. What I learned here in this station is that certain things like having crushed testicles or a history of venereal disease, or a heart murmur, or being flatfooted, or conditions like severe acne are all disqualifying, or at least they were then. Ditto for being a fatty or a stick man. I heard later in the war some of these conditions were no longer disqualifying.

The next subcomponent of Phase III was a vision test. Do you have 20-20 vision? I did. If not, how bad is it? What I saw here was guys with coke bottle lenses getting turned away. Other guys with glasses with normal lenses were passed. I never knew where they drew the line. They also checked you for colorblindness, which was another disqualifier. From what I observed, most guys passed.

Next was hearing. They examined inside your ears like you had a hornets nest hidden in there. They put you in a soundproof booth and wanted to know if you could hear certain sounds. There was a thick glass window you looked through and gave them a thumbs up if you heard it. I think they asked a couple of times when there wasn't a sound, just to see if you were faking it. Anyway, I passed. That was all I did on the second day because the lines were long.

The third day I continued in Phase III with the fourth subcomponent. This was the dental examination. Inductees had to have 18 natural teeth which were healthy. Fortunately, dental hygiene had been stressed in my family, so this was an easy test for me. I saw several who didn't pass this portion - one had dentures - and it surprised me.

The last subcomponent for Phase III was psychiatric. Nobody with any history of mental illness was accepted. They also played some type of head game on you which was designed to anger you to see if you could handle the pressure. Would you fold or lash out? If you did either, you were done.

That was it. It took three full days, of which a major factor of time consumption was standing in line waiting your turn. You know the old Army adage, "Hurry up and wait." It's true.

While I was in line, I had a lot of time on my hands to observe folks. All the men in line were there because they wanted to right the wrongs which had been perpetrated on us by the Japanese. That now included the Nazis and all the other Axis Powers. Most of the guys were solid. They were all patriots. That being said, there are always a few blowhards - the kind of guys you wish would just shut their traps. I tried to avoid them if I could.

I noticed there seemed to be two major concerns among the prospective enlistees. First and foremost, was being rejected. I was definitely included in that group. The other was this. Although everyone there wanted to do his patriotic duty, quite a few only had one branch in mind.

I'd say most were like me. They wanted Army; however, many considered that a low bar. Those were the guys who wanted (Army) Air Force, Navy, or Marine Corps. I didn't see anyone who wanted Coast Guard, but there might've been some there. They were probably the smart guys who kept their traps shut and didn't pontificate.

The Army bashers pointed out that the guys who passed all the tests, but were rejected by the other branches, all wound up in the Army. It was absolutely true. I reckon that means the Army is for ordinary joes and the other branches are for extraordinary joes.

That being said, not everyone here would get a primary designation with a frontline combat role, no matter which branch he got. All the bloviators professed to a burning desire to kill as many of our nation's enemies as they could. I wondered if they had ever seen someone die a violent death. I also wondered if they had ever been in a life-or-death situation themselves. Some of them would get something less glamorous than what they professed to desire. Not all football players are ball handlers. Some are interior linemen. Not everyone here would get a frontline tasking no matter how big a badass they thought they were. Maybe they would be the lucky ones after all.

A shoe clerk is still a shoe clerk no matter which uniform he wears. He has value too, just like an aviator, boat driver, grunt rifleman, engineer, or artilleryman. America needed them all. In fact, more than one shoe clerk has risen all the way up to major general or rear admiral. Usually only their peers know who they are. It's pointless and tacky to throw stones at your teammates and allies. Fighter pilot, submarine commander, paratrooper, Marine Corps recon - they all need shoes, beans, bullets, gear, and transportation. You get the point, but some didn't. The Marine wannabes were the absolute worst. Can you spell arrogant? I hoped they got exactly what they wished for.

Anyway, three days had elapsed, and finally my testing was complete. They sent me home. I knew I had passed. They said I'd be notified by mail. They didn't say when. I woulda thought time was of the essence.

I guess it was. On Monday, December 29th, I received my induction notice for the Army. I was ordered to report to the Louisville Armory at 0800 hours on Wednesday, January 7th. They clearly stated that personal belongings were limited to what you were wearing, plus a shaving kit and Bible; however, they said they'd issue both and they did. All I brought was a toothbrush. The Bible was a shirt pocket size New Testament printed by the Gideons. I still have it.

On Tuesday, I notified my sergeant, captain, and LPD Personnel. It was real important. If I returned alive with an honorable discharge, they had to give me my old job back, just like I had never been gone. It was the law. I wasn't the only guy on the job in Louisville who served in the armed forces during WWII. I was just the first to go. My last day was a bittersweet parting.

I took the next seven days off to spend it with my family. It was high time to make some lasting memories. Who knew when I would see them again? It was another bittersweet parting. Fear of the unknown can be paralyzing. I put on my bravest face so the kids wouldn't panic. Papa and Chloe both helped me in that endeavor. Poor Mama was having a hard time holding it together.

-9-
My Time in the Service

I reported for induction as ordered. I was one of 160 Army recruits there that day. We were assembled into different sections, each under the command of a corporal. Then we were sworn in by a commissioned officer. The corporal gave each recruit a paper tag, bearing his last name, first name, and middle initial in that order, with a string to wear it around his neck. Failure to wear it properly resulted in unwanted attention and a serious blessing out.

My group of 36 was taken by bus to the train station. Corporal Alfred T. Ledbetter was in charge. He was the last to board with us. He made a roll call at each pitstop along the way to make sure no man was left behind, especially once we boarded the train.

We disembarked three days later in Monterey, California, worn out and full of anxiety. We were met by Staff Sergeant Honus M. Butler and Corporal Theodore J. Compton, our drill instructor (DI) and assistant drill instructor (ADI), respectively. It was painfully obvious that they ate nails for breakfast. For darn sure they could breathe fire. It seemed like they were always angry, and shouting at the top of their lungs. They had eagle eyes, and caught every faux pas made by an errant recruit. However, in all fairness, if a recruit performed some task in an exemplary manner, they also acknowledged it publicly. Sometimes that was even worse.

Corporal Ledbetter bade us adieu and made arrangements

to return to Louisville. I never saw him again. At this point he seemed mild, compared to our new mama and papa.

Our new exacting parents boarded us on an Army bus headed to Fort Ord, home of the 7th Infantry Division, and our new corporate identity. We were its newest members. Corporal Compton handed each of us a dozen 7th Division patches to sew on the left upper shoulder of our shirt and coat sleeves - that is - once we were issued clothing. This included a few spares. The patches were a two-inch, red circle with a black border. They had a black hourglass in the middle. My understanding is the 7th Infantry Division was comprised mostly of activated California National Guardsmen, so we were the outsiders, being from Kentucky. We were taken to a new recruit basic training area on the outskirts of Fort Ord proper called Camp Clayton.

We completed 12 weeks of infantry basic training on April 3rd. We graduated 34. They discovered Private Franks was queer and sent him packing with a Dishonorable Discharge. Private Ellis broke his back on the obstacle course. The last we heard he was still in an Army hospital. None of us ever expected to see him again and we didn't.

Upon graduation, we were split up into three different infantry regiments. Some went to the 17th; some went to the 23rd; and, six of us went to the 159th, all subcomponents of the 7th Infantry Division. FYI - Regiments are commanded by a colonel. Divisions are commanded by a major general.

At the time we graduated, the 7th Infantry Division was known as the 7th Motorized Infantry Division, but that only lasted a year. Later they took away the trucks, so we reverted back to light infantry with our old name. When we went to war, we would go on our feet with whatever we could carry on our backs.

Anyway, as soon as our new assignments were posted, we were allowed to depart on two weeks leave. Travel to and from came out of your own pocket.

My reunion with family was joyful beyond words. Time slipped through my fingers like running water. The kids seemed so much bigger and stronger. Chloe was more beautiful than ever. She was also especially attentive to me. I ate that up. Mama looked the same as she always did. I could see she was content, in spite of missing me.

Papa seemed much older. He was 72 now, and the arthritis was really bothering him. He seemed a little stooped. I was secretly worried about him, but didn't let on. He was especially proud of me because I shot Expert with the M-1 Garand rifle, and because I got promoted to Pfc (private first class). I was no longer a 'slick sleeve' Pvt. Now I wore one chevron on each sleeve. I told him being twice as old as the rest of the recruits gave me a leg up, but he didn't want to hear it. The truth is, age gave me wisdom the youngsters didn't have yet. I could see trouble coming long before they could, so I was able to avoid it most of the time.

One day Papa and I drove to HQ so I could say hello to my old police pals. I learned that eleven officers were now in the armed forces. Everyone said they missed me, and told me to keep my head down.

My time evaporated like a raindrop in the desert. I had to board the train back to Fort Ord. Upon arrival, I met up with all 33 classmates. Everyone's batteries had been recharged.

We spent one night at Camp Clayton. The next morning,

we drew our rifles and TA-50 (tactical assault gear). We ate an early lunch and boarded two M-35, 2-1/2-ton, 6x6 diesel trucks, otherwise known in Army parlance as a deuce-and-a-half, for transportation to a remote training ground in the Mojave Desert near Bakersfield, California. The trip was 250 miles. That is a very long ride bouncing around on a wooden plank seat in the back of a deuce-and-a-half, but it beat marching.

The M-35 is a gigantic, overgrown pickup truck with a canvas top over the back and the roof of the cab. The storage area, or bed, has a bench on each side running front to rear. Each bench can hold ten infantrymen and their tactical gear. It's driven by an enlisted troop. That's his full-time Army job. The commanding sergeant or officer-in-charge rides in the front right seat.

During our absence on leave, that's when the Army decided the 7th ID (Infantry Division) would be deployed to the African Theater, which is why we trained in the desert. It made oodles of sense.

We trained for eight arduous months, in the 100+ degree heat with nearly no humidity. I learned how to cope with concrete buggers in my nose, and wear goggles for hours on end to keep the blowing sand out of my eyes. We ran in formation, conducted more obstacle course drills, completed small unit (light infantry) tactics, and spent days on the range, honing in our rifle marksmanship skills, and learning how to disassemble, clean, and shoot the M-2 Browning coaxial machine gun, M1918 Browning Automatic Rifle (BAR), M-1 bazooka (2.46-inch rocket launcher), M-2 60-millimeter mortar, and increase our range and accuracy with the Mk-2 fragmentation hand grenade, nicknamed the pineapple because of its appearance. We didn't waste anymore time on bayonet drills. Did I say I'd much rather be shot than stabbed?

I went from 153 pounds to 141, but we were all in tiptop shape for desert fighting and ready to go to war in Africa. They promoted me to corporal and made me an assistant squad leader. I was gung-ho, full of piss and vinegar. You could say I was in my element.

During this time, on June 3, 1942, the Japanese made another sneak attack on American soil, similar to the one on Pearl Harbor, except this time it included a ground invasion.

It took place in the Aleutian Islands in the Territory of Alaska. For two days they bombed the Dutch Harbor Naval Operating Base, and its next-door Army neighbor, Fort Mears. Their primary targets were the naval radio station and the petroleum storage tanks. Two days later they landed troops on Kiska Island, and the next day they captured Attu Island, both of which were also in the Aleutians. They immediately built garrisons at both sites. Estimated total strength of the Japanese ground forces was 7,000 troops.

We read about this, like we did other battles, such as the Battle of Midway, which occurred during the same period of time, but we were busy training for desert warfare to fight in Africa. This was another black eye for America, and we were concerned, but at the same time, we had bigger fish to fry. Basically we forgot all about it. Not our problem. Some other division would have to deal with it.

Then in January of 1943, we experienced another radical change. Someone with lots of stars on his collar decided, no, the 7th would be deployed to the Pacific, instead of Africa.

That's actually when we lost our wheels and reverted back to light infantry, forevermore to be called the 7th Infantry Division. No more Motorized for us. I can only surmise it is easier to drive trucks in the desert than in the jungle.

So in January of 1943, we dumped desert warfare and began rigorous amphibious assault training under the tutelage of the Fleet Marine Force in another remote location. I think it was in an area known as 19 Palms, but they never said. That was just a rumor. All I know for certain is we were still in California. The U.S. Marines were considered the experts in amphibious assault. This was their baby. It was a little tough putting up with the Marine Corps' arrogant attitude, but I confess, they taught us well. By then, I had been on active duty a year and had never heard a shot fired in anger, although I had been trained very well to shoot my issue M-1 Garand rifle out to 450 yards.

One day in January, I think it was the 16th, we were in ranks during morning muster. Every soldier and gyrene there who didn't already have one, was awarded the American Campaign Medal, so long as he had 12 or more consecutive months of military service since December 7, 1941, all of which occurred within the borders of the United States and/or any of the oceans during World War II. Actually what they handed out was the ribbon, with the full medal coming down the pike later. Troops in the European-African-Middle Eastern Theater and the Asiatic Pacific Theater were awarded different colored campaign ribbons with different time requirements, but we hadn't seen any of those. I was real proud of my ribbon and always wore it when we were in Class As (dress uniform).

I'll assume you want to know what it looks like. The American Campaign Medal was attached to a medium blue ribbon with thin vertical white, red, black, and white stripes clustered on each side, and a very thin vertical blue, white, and red striped cluster down the middle. It was a bronze, 1-1/4-inch disk. The obverse depicts a Navy cruiser underway with a sinking enemy submarine in the foreground, and a B-24 Liberator flying overhead. The reverse depicts a perched American bald eagle and the words *United States of America.*

Man plans. God laughs. This time He probably laughed 'til he cried.

As soon as we received our ribbons, we were ordered to go back to our barracks and pack up everything. We were going to war! Everybody let out a spontaneous cheer. Once we calmed down, the colonel said, "To Alaska, you boneheads! You go where the Army needs you most! Get the lead out! We depart in three hours! Dismissed!"

After eight months of desert training and five months of amphibious attack training, also in 100-degree weather, we were scrambled to the cold and snow and ice of Alaska. Talk about grumbling and confusion! Almost overnight, we deployed to the North Pacific, acclimatized for the heat in deserts and jungles, but without proper winter warfare garments or footwear. This was a low ebb for all of us. Being in a leadership role, I tried to make the most of it.

The Army had a special train laid on just for us 7th Infantry Division heroes. Then we boarded a troop ship in San Francisco. We sailed to Anchorage, where we disembarked. Altogether, it took us ten days to arrive. We heard later that the Army had beefed up to 94,000 troops in Alaska, but that's hard for me to believe. I never saw anything near that many. Darn near all the sleeve patches I saw were 7th Infantry Division.

We trained some more. It was a darn good thing too, because we needed to acclimatize. I slowly grew accustomed to the snow and cold, but I never liked it. I was an assistant squad leader, and it was incumbent upon me to lead from the front. My squad leader, Sergeant Harry K. Purvis from Mississippi, was a great guy. Our platoon sergeant, Sergeant First Class Avery M. Nixon, was from Oakland, California. Our platoon leader, 2nd Lieutenant Oscar G. Blevins, was from Costa Mesa, California. Our company commander, Captain Everett B. Sloan, was from Los Angeles, California. These were all outstanding men, and I didn't want to let any of them down. None of us had ever been in combat, but I believe being a police officer for 17 years, I was the only one in this group who had ever shot someone, let alone killed someone. I knuckled down and did everything I could do to set the example.

We trained with the 17th Infantry Regiment. I wasn't sure why, but I knew it had to mean something. I didn't think it happened by accident.

On May 5th, 1943, we boarded a troop ship. It took us off the coast of Attu Island, where we prepared to board Higgins boats to make the amphibious attack. Our amphibious attack training paid off then, many thanks to the Marines. Climbing down the rope nets encumbered with our packs, rifles, and everything else we could manage was not easy, especially with the rocking of the ship and landing craft, not to mention the deplorable cold, windy, and rainy weather.

They called this Operation Landcrab.

The Canadian Air Force had made reconnaissance flights and strafing runs. The U.S. Navy had conducted massive bombardments. The Japs knew without a doubt that we were coming. They had plenty of time to prepare a reception for us!

On May 11th, we initiated our attack. We landed 11,000 total troops divided between the north and south ends of the island. I was in the southern group. I was scared out of my mind, but I had men to lead. I sucked it up. We were dealing with arctic weather (in May!), but on this particular day, I didn't even notice. I did later. We had scores of soldiers who were casualties due to cold weather related injuries.

My boat was not in the first wave. We were somewhere in the middle. We thought for sure the bombardment had knocked out the worst of the enemy's entrenched defenses, but the reality we faced indicated otherwise. We fought for every inch of ground, and we incurred a lot of casualties. Lieutenant Blevins was the first to die in our platoon. Death came from a machine gun emplacement. When Private Keith Collins knocked it out with the bazooka, it didn't do much to ease my pain. It just meant this particular crew wasn't going to get me.

The island was a mostly treeless, rocky, volcanic wasteland. The wind was fearsome, and the rain was pounding. This was January or February weather back home. We knocked out foxhole after foxhole, continuously pushing forward. We had to keep moving, not just to kill the enemy, but to stay as warm as possible. We were told the battle would be over in three days, but God laughed again and it took 19.

On May 23rd, I got grazed by a round in my left calf. It

took out a big chunk of meat. A medic treated me with a powdered sulfur disinfectant, and bandaged me up. I quickly rejoined what was left of my platoon. It hurt, but I was too cold to feel much pain. I guess that was a blessing.

We slept wherever we could find shelter. Our supply trains had a hard time catching up with us. We were always cold, hungry, and worn out, and it seemed like we were always wet.

On May 29th, the Japs massed in overwhelming numbers and came right through us like a lightning bolt in a thunderstorm. This was a complete surprise - a terrifying banzai charge. I had heard about them.

Everyone in camp from the frontline fighters to the cooks and company clerks in the rear grabbed a rifle and fought for their lives. There had to be a thousand or more! Fortunately, many of the enemy had run out of ammunition, and were relying on their bayonets, which were attached to their rifles. They were crazed like they were high on some type of amphetamine. I have no idea how many I shot that day. Dozens at least. The most notable was a Jap charging Captain Sloan from behind. I shot him three times. He finally fell, just before he could bury his bayonet into Captain Sloan's back. He looked up at me and smiled.

Later on, I was awarded the Army Commendation with a V-device for valor due to Captain Sloan's recommendation. Not that I was pursuing a rack of medals, they're nice, but I soon realized a soldier could perform a dozen deeds of derring-do, but if no one witnessed it, particularly an important someone, it's like it never happened. It happened to me several times. That's why the grizzly veterans are more impressed with campaign medals with campaign stars than the medals for personal valor. It's a matter of record who fought in a campaign. Acts of valor are more commonplace than a non-vet would imagine, but most of them go unnoticed or officially unrecognized.

I later learned we killed 2,800 enemy soldiers that one day. That was the last hurrah for them. We won. I felt ecstatic and depressed all at the same time. We lost 550 men, not counting those wounded or injured, out of 11,000 who were there. Only 30 Japs surrendered and were taken prisoner.

I didn't know it yet, but my combat days were over.

We had a lot of vacancies in our company. Captain Sloan promoted me to sergeant when he gave me the Purple Heart and Commendation Medal. I was honored in more ways than one.

We recouped, filled empty ranks, and went back to training. Our regiment was not involved in the amphibious attack on Kiska Island, but that turned out to be a bust anyway. Unbeknownst to us, the Japs had already vacated the premises. That meant all the Japs had been killed or expelled from the Territory of Alaska. We were ready to move on. Say adiós amigo to Alaska. Go somewhere warm. Didn't happen. No indeed.

On August 23, 1943, we were transferred to the Alaskan Department. It became our permanent mission to protect Alaska from further Japanese incursions. It was a big letdown on the one hand, and a relief on the other. It was doubtful we'd see more combat in Alaska, now that we were finally outfitted to fight there with arctic garments and boots.

We remained for a year as an indigenous unit within the

Alaskan Departmental TO&E (Table of Organization & Equipment). Altogether, we served in Alaska for 19 months. It was the longest we ever stayed anywhere. Just before we left, I was promoted to staff sergeant. Besides being an infantry squad leader, now I was segundo to the platoon sergeant. I took over for him whenever he was absent. Heck. I'd already been doing it unofficially for six months.

On August 9, 1944, we departed by ship to Seattle. It took 11 days. From there we went to Camp Swift, Texas, near Bastrop, arriving August 28. It was both a training camp and a German POW stockade. Nobody knew why we were there. We weren't an MP (Military Police) unit with an MOS (Military Occupational Specialty) of 95-C, trained to be stockade guards. Ergo, we trained more in small unit infantry tactics. By now we all knew the drill well. We'd seen combat. We also knew all about the Invasion of Normandy on June 6, 1944, and the island-hopping campaign in the Pacific. Basically, we were in limbo, and didn't understand why.

They kept bouncing us around again and again. On December 28, 1944, they moved us to Camp Callan, near San Diego. This was a replacement depot. It led us to believe we were headed for the Pacific Theater. We sat on our thumbs waiting for orders.

Son of a gun, if they didn't sent us right back to Camp Swift on January 28, 1945!

I was really sick when we arrived, so they checked me into the infirmary. I had double pneumonia. I was completely out of commission for a month, and even then I was still weak.

On February 27, 1945, before I was released from the hospital, what remained of the 7th Infantry Division left for

Camp Kilmer, New Jersey. They left without me. It sort of wigged me out. I'd spent the last three years with them. I felt a little abandoned. The war wasn't over yet.

They shipped out on March 7, 1945, arriving in France on March 18th. At this time, the 7th ID only consisted of two regiments - the 23rd and 159th. Both were attached to augment the 106th Infantry Division, which had been decimated in the Battle of the Bulge.

They arrived in Germany on April 25, 1945. That was five days before Adolf Hitler committed suicide. Germany surrendered on May 8.

On November 4, 1945, the 7th Infantry Division disembarked in New York City. They were transported to Camp Shanks, New York, where the 7th was deactivated.

I was honorably discharged effective March 25, 1945. My DD-214 (Certificate of Release or Discharge from Active Duty) and DD-215 (Correction to DD Form 214, Certificate of Uniformed Service) reflect that I was awarded the Combat Infantryman's Badge (CIB), Army Commendation Medal with V Device, Purple Heart, Good Conduct Medal, American Campaign Medal with one campaign star (for the Aleutians campaign), the World War II Victory Medal, and the Honorable Discharge Lapel Pin, referred to as the Ruptured Duck (to wear on my civvies). Not all of the medals were given to me when I walked out the door, but I had the ribbons. The rest of the medals were mailed to me after the war ended.

When I departed Camp Swift, I was wearing a brand new wool dress uniform. It consisted of OD trousers, 'Ike Jacket' with the 7th ID shoulder patch, and garrison cap. The long sleeve shirt, tie, and web belt with brass buckle were all tan. We wore brown, low quarter shoes. I was wearing my CIB and every ribbon I earned, except for the WWII Victory Medal, which had not come out yet. The tailors had already sewn the yellow cloth Ruptured Duck above my right breast pocket, one diagonal three-year service stripe on my left sleeve, and three, horizontal six-month overseas stripes on the right sleeve. I was gaunt, but I thought I looked real spiffy in my new duds. I was real proud to wear them.

I was glad I served, and even gladder to be honorably discharged.

-10-
Homecoming

Before I boarded the train in Bastrop, I stopped by the Western Union office in the train station, and sent a telegram to Chloe. I told her I would arrive on the train from Memphis at 11:25 o'clock, the evening of March 10. That was a Saturday night. I said I would catch a taxi if she couldn't meet me. I couldn't wait to get home. I had two weeks of terminal leave with pay.

I was worn out when we pulled into the station. Anxious though I was to see Chloe, I was moving very slowly. The pneumonia and the trip had sapped all my strength. I was one of the last from my carriage to disembark.

My luggage consisted of a quarter-full duffle bag. I doubt it weighed 15 pounds. I saw them, the whole family, including Mama and Papa, brother Angus, Jr., his wife Carla and their three kids, sister Phoebe and her two kids, Theodore's wife, Abigail and his son, and of course my sweet Chloe, Arnie, and Arabella, even before I began to walk down the steps. I was overwhelmed and couldn't contain myself. I started gushing tears of joy.

They all ran up to me. Junior took my bag, and they all, one-by-one, gave me a big hug. It had been nearly three years since I had seen them. I could tell they could hardly recognize me because I had lost 20 pounds.

We all went back to Mama's house for sandwiches, chocolate cake with vanilla ice cream, and soft drinks for some, and Old Doctor Crow for the menfolk. Papa got out his old Kodak and began snapping pictures. I insisted on taking some with him in them. The party didn't break up until 2:30. This may very well have been the best day of my life.

Chloe made over me like I was an injured lost puppy. She fed me like I was a survivor from a concentration camp. She did all she could to put some meat on my rack of bones. I began to get well and regain my strength.

I got caught up on all the family news.

Papa was 75 years old and in declining health. He was having a difficult time getting around with the arthritis. He couldn't mow the grass or tend to the shrubs anymore. Arnie was taking care of that. He couldn't garden. Mama and Chloe were doing that. He seldom felt up to going to church. He had been a faithful attendee for as long as I could remember. Mostly he sat in his easy chair and read the *Courier Journal* newspaper and listened to the radio, particularly the Cincinnati Reds baseball games, but also the U. of L. basketball games, and of course the news. He didn't eat much. He fell asleep in his chair every afternoon. The good news is he was cheerful and had all his faculties.

Mama was 73, but she was as spry as a goosed rabbit. She and Chloe did nearly everything together. They were tighter than two coats of paint. Being that we lived with Mama and Phoebe did not, Chloe had pretty much taken over Phoebe's roll in her younger days before she married.

Junior was 47. When the war began he was aged out. Now he was an engineer, filling Papa's shoes at the L&N Railroad. He and Carla and the three kids came around to visit a lot.

Phoebe was 45. She was also a working mom. She and her

husband, Hiram, worked in their bakery six days a week. They had a thriving business. Their two kids mostly grew up in the bakery. Hiram was 50, so he was also aged out when the war began.

Claude was 44. He'd been in the Navy since he was 18. Now he was a chief petty officer, as high as an enlisted man can go. He'd served in the Pacific his entire career as a boatswain's mate on numerous cruisers and destroyers. A boatswain's mate is a deckhand, which is the backbone of any seagoing vessel.

He'd been in four major battles during the war, including Pearl Harbor, Midway, Coral Sea, and the Solomon Islands. He had been awarded the Navy Commendation Medal, two Purple Hearts, and six Good Conduct Medals. No doubt he was tougher than a boiled kangaroo hide.

Claude had never married.

He claimed he had a tattoo of Popeye the Sailor on the inside of his left forearm and chief petty officer stripes on his left upper arm (where they would be stitched on). He also said when he retired, he planned to remain in Hawaii. Honolulu was his home now when he wasn't on board a vessel. He said he might even sign on with the U.S. Merchant Marine so he could continue sailing, not to mention earning money. He hadn't been home since his leave in 1919, after basic training in Great Lakes, Illinois. He did send Mama an official military photograph of him in his dress whites when he got promoted to chief petty officer. It took place on board a ship. We were all very proud of him, but we didn't know him anymore. He'd been gone too long. There had never been any bad blood between the family and him. I reckon it was just too far to travel here from San Francisco or Honolulu.

Theodore, also known as Teddy, was a year older than me. Somehow he managed to get selected for the Army Air Force right after I reported for active duty. He was a turret gunner in a B-17 Flying Fortress in the 8th Air Force, which was stationed in England. He was awarded an Air Medal during the invasion of Normandy on D-Day. He was still over there fighting the war when I arrived home, hoping to be discharged soon. During his stint overseas, his wife Abigail and his son, Kermit, moved back in with her folks.

Arnie was 15, and a sophomore at Male High School. He was making good grades. He had a part-time job as a bag-boy at Gleason's Market a block from the house, except during the school's baseball season, March through May. He didn't make the team last year, but this year he did. He was the second string catcher.

Arabella was 11. She was in the 6th grade. She was also our precocious, academic child. Her primary responsibility around the house, besides helping her grandma and mama, was to take care of all the cat's needs. The cat was a black American shorthair with white underwear and stockings, three years old. She slept on Annabella's bed. Her name was Sweetness.

That pretty much sums up my entire family the day I returned home from the war in March of 1945.

On March 26, 1945, when my terminal military leave was up, I girded myself in my old police uniform, which hung off of me like it belonged to the fat man in the circus. I took the bus instead of walking. There were a lot of new faces, but fortunately a few from my past, too.

I took my Form DD-214, and marched right in to Personnel like I'd never been gone. I presented myself to Patrolman Leland M. Roe. He was an old timer with 26 years on the job. A criminal's bullet from a liquor store robbery when I was a young pup left him with a gimpy leg. That's how come he was a beancounter now. Nevertheless, he was a good egg. He made the most out of his disability, and he had a soft spot for foot patrolmen such as my flatfoot self.

He greeted me warmly while he pulled my personnel file from the cabinet. He said I looked like Hell, and wanted to know if I were on a starvation diet. I replied that I had just recovered from pneumonia, but was feeling fine now. Then he started perusing my Form DD-214 like it was a pornographic book with lots of pictures in color.

He said, "Alaska, huh? How was that?"

"Every bit as cold as you can imagine and then some. As you can see for yourself, I was there 19 months. Eventually, I got used to it - almost."

"No wonder you're so bony. Dern! CIB and Purple Heart. Commendation Medal for Valor. Staff Sergeant in three years. I'd say you did very well for yourself. Congratulations on a job well done."

Then he reached across the desk and shook my hand.

I replied, "Thanks."

He said, "There's one thing you gotta do right away, and another you should do. Whaddaya want first?"

"Easiest thing first."

"No problem. You were on an unpaid leave of absence for 3 years, 2 months, and 19 days. Since then we received two raises. You'll be happy to hear that if you want all that time to count towards your retirement, you'll need to pay the city whatever portion you would have paid into the retirement system during that time, had you been paid. It's 7% of whatever you would have earned. You don't have to pay any interest on it if you make full reimbursement within a year.

"I can ballpark it in my head. It's going to be about $250. It shouldn't be more than that. You can do it by payroll deduction in equal installments. That would run you roughly $10 per check. You can pay it in a lump sum. You can kiss it off altogether and lose all that time. It's up to you."

"How do I do it by payroll deduction?"

"I thought you'd never ask. Sign this form here. Payroll will do the math. They'll send you a letter. Each paycheck the debit will be annotated on your paystub. When it's paid off in full, they'll annotate your retirement account and send you a letter. Keep it in your personal files at home in case they have a SNAFU (Army acronym for Situation normal. All fucked up.) and don't factor the debt paid when they go to figure your retirement."

I signed the form. "What's the harder thing?"

Leland passed me another form and smiled. "You know Old Doc Snyder down the street. Walk over there and let him check you out to make sure you're good to return back on the street again. He'll fill out this form and sign it. Bring it back to me. I'll give you a chit to take to Captain Dithers. You remember him. Good boss. He's Chief of Patrol now. He'll put you back to work. Hopefully you'll be back on the bricks serving the public by lunchtime."

The medical examination was no heavy lifting. Doc Snyders turned a blind eye to me being six pounds underweight. I brought the signed form back to Leland. He gave me a chit. I went to see Captain Oswald G. Dithers in his office.

Captain Dithers greeted me warmly. He assigned me to Day Shift on a walking beat in the CBD close to our home. In fact, it was my same old beat, number 7. He knew that. He apologized that he didn't have a motorized beat open right now. I assured him that I was pleased with my new posting, and I truly was.

He said the Department was growing by leaps and bounds and it wouldn't be long before we'd be creating four new police districts with their own buildings, separate from the CBD, which would continue to report out of HQ; further, there would be a lot of new supervisory positions to be filled. It was 1945, and this was the beginning of a new era. He even got me excited about the changes. This was a new revelation for a conservative such as me.

He handed me a pamphlet with information about what was required to get promoted to patrol sergeant. He wanted me to study it so I could pass the written exam. He said he had something in mind for me. I thanked him and promised to bone up.

We were done. It was noon, so I left to return to work on Beat 7, with a great big dog-eating-poop grin spread across my mug. I had been gone way too long. It was great to be back in the briar patch. I could hardly wait to tell Chloe.

My new status quo continued uneventfully for several months. I picked up 10 pounds, and not all around my waist! I got my legs back in shape with all the walking, but do confess, I was never again in as good of shape as I had been in during my tenure in the Mohave Desert. That was my pinnacle of physical fitness. I had been a 'lean, green, fighting machine'.

Teddy was discharged from the Army Air Force in late July. We had another reunion like mine, except Papa didn't appear to be his old self. Everyone could see it. He passed away in his sleep on August 7th. It was like he waited for Teddy to return home. Papa's death rocked our world.

Everyone except for Claude came to the funeral, and he sent a telegram.

We bought a plot in Cave Hill Cemetery for Papa and Mama. The Veterans of Foreign Wars provided an honor guard. The Kentucky National Guard sent a team to fold the American flag, which they presented to Mama. The American Legion knew who to contact to get a military bronze footplate to place in front of his tombstone. It took nearly a year to get. It read, *Private Angus R. Sinclair, 1870-1945, Company H, 1st Kentucky Volunteer Infantry Regiment, Puerto Rico, 1898-1899.*

We eventually moved on with our lives because you have to. It was awfully quiet around the house for many days. Once Mama wasn't thinking and put out a place setting for Papa at supper. Nobody said a word. Every now and then I'd be thinking about him and tear up. I was a full-grown man 41 years old, and he had always been there for me. Now he wasn't. I couldn't imagine Mama's pain.

One day when I was out in the backyard alone, she slipped up on me and caught me silently weeping. She put her hand on my shoulder and softly spoke, "Don't weep for Papa. His time on Earth has passed. All his pain is gone. He's up in Heaven with Jesus. Someday we will all meet Papa up there.

He's at peace now, smiling down on us, hoping we live our lives to the fullest. You need his prayers, but he doesn't need yours anymore. He's living the life now that we all seek, and are promised by Jesus Christ Himself. Understand?"

"Understand."

I still missed him daily, but my pain didn't seem as great.

I made a 95 on the sergeant's examination. I was number 2 on the list. It was Friday, October 5th. The Department was marking time, waiting for the four new district stations to be renovated from existing buildings, and then to be furnished.

Finally the station in the West End was completed. LPD command was impatiently waiting for the others to be finished. They were all ready on Wednesday, November 21st, the day before Thanksgiving. On Friday, the list of promotions was posted. I got Day Shift patrol sergeant in the CBD. Promotions were effective Monday, December 3rd. Merry Christmas came early for all who were knighted!

The Department now boasted 161 sworn officers, and they still weren't done hiring. They planned to increase staffing up to 200. There were 13 new sergeants, five new lieutenants, four new captains, and one new major - Captain Dithers, whose position as Chief of Patrol, was upgraded. Chief Leonard E. Duckworth was promoted from Major to Colonel. We didn't have a lieutenant colonel.

They had a massive swearing in ceremony on Monday, the 3rd, and all the wives were invited. Mayor Cornelius B. Peabody presided, himself. It was a gala affair with orange sherbet punch, coffee, and a variety of assorted cookies and iced cupcakes. Chloe looked ravishing in her new dress and heels. She was duly impressed by the pomp and circumstance. We'd never seen anything like this before. The City of Louisville really put on the dog. The *Courier Journal* even sent out a reporter and a photographer. Second time ever for my mug to be in the newspaper.

All new promotees received a complete new issue of uniforms. For sergeants, this included a tunic with gold sergeant stripes on the sleeves, and for me, five matching gold seniority stripes on the bottom of the left sleeve; also, six white shirts with gold sergeant stripes, three pairs of trousers which actually fit, two black ties, and upgraded cap with a gold hatband. We also received a new gold-plated badge, hat shield and ID card.

The CBD still had four walking beats, but as a sergeant, I had a marked unit so I could check up on my patrolmen. I shared it with the CBD patrol sergeants on the other two shifts. It was one of the newer vehicles - a black and white, 1941 Studebaker Champion with 53,000 honest miles on it. It ran really well. They had quit making new cars during the war, so everyone had to make do with what they already had. HQ figured there wouldn't be very many new automobiles rolling off the assembly lines until sometime in 1947.

I wasn't complaining. I had a set of wheels and it was in great shape - better than my old flivver. Besides, Papa drove it way more than I ever did. It was more his jalopy than mine.

It didn't take as long as you'd think. By the time 1946 rolled around, it was almost like I had never been gone. Life was nearly back to normal.

-11-
Rolling Forward

Times were good, very good, the rest of the 1940s up until 1953. That year was a double whammy. First, Arnie was killed in action on July 6th in Korea, and then Mama passed away from a heart attack on Friday, November 27th. It was the day after Thanksgiving. Maybe I'll touch on this later. Right now, their deaths are still too painful for me to talk about.

I never aspired for rank on the Police Department. I liked my job as a foot patrolman. I had no interest in ensconcing myself in HQ in an office with a padded chair, brown-nosing my superiors, sipping on coffee all day long, and waiting for the worker bees to call in for assignments. Ditto re making beat assignments, writing evaluations, or dealing with irate citizens who were unhappy with how a patrolman performed his job. Just give me a patch of turf to patrol and I'll do it happily as long as I'm able.

I guess to some degree, World War II shifted my parameters. I still liked walking a beat, being the face of LPD to the citizens on my beat, arresting scoundrels, and trying to make a positive impact one-on-one, face-to-face with our fellow taxpayers. However, I had tasted rank and responsibility in the Army with troops who for the most part were half my age, and I enjoyed it. It was almost like being a father figure to them.

Now that I was a patrol sergeant, I could have the best of both worlds, and I did. I spent most of my days out on the street, backing up my men, maintaining contact with the public, except now my turf had expanded to four beats. Life was great. I'd be okay, so long as I didn't shine so well that they wanted to promote me to lieutenant, which is a position stuck inside the building administrating files without faces. Besides, at this stage of my life, it would have been tough for me taking orders from a 30-year-old who was still wet behind the ears. The Job kept getting better and better, and at the same time, our family flourished, except for 1953. That year it did not. Still, what more could an honest man ask for?

Getting back to potential assassins, earlier I said I had a half dozen possible suspects gleaned from my personal files. I mentioned three - Delbert S. Finnegan, Lonnie Joseph Butts, and Gordon T. Bertram. The fourth is a guy named Rufus H. Dorman.

He and his running buddy, Bradley F. Townsend, were a couple of stickup artists from across the river in New Albany, Indiana. In 1953, I had a chance encounter with them and another mutt, Howard K. Boggs, who was Townsend's cousin. It was the week after we buried Arnie.

I guess you could say my heart was broken and my compassion for Mankind was at an all time low ebb. It was their misfortune to tangle assholes with me (sorry for my profanity but I can't come up with a more benign description with the same impact) during my time of grief. I've thought about this since then several times, but the results always come out the same.

These brainiacs were already wanted by the Indiana State Police, Floyd County, Indiana Sheriff's Office, and the New Albany Police Department for three counts of armed robbery.

I suppose they decided to drive across the Ohio River on the 2nd Street Bridge and raid the Derby City, just like the Yankee Army did back in 1861 - just for the sheer fun of it.

Howard K. Boggs was an addendum to their group. He was the wheelman after the second robbery, which allowed Dorman and Townsend to cover each other when they entered a business to frighten honest folks while they pillaged it. As of this time, they hadn't drawn blood.

They decided to rob Broadway Liquors next to the Greyhound Bus Station at Broadway and 8th Street. They selected the most prosperous liquor store in all of the CBD. Anyone with eyes could see that this establishment was raking in cash by the bucketsful.

I was trying out our brand new, marked 1953 Chevrolet Bel Air sedan. I just happened to be stopped for the traffic light on Broadway at 8th when I saw two men with masks and handguns come pell mell out of the liquor store. The bandit in the blue checked shirt also had a brown paper grocery sack in his left hand.

Mr. Schlisser, the proprietor, followed them out the door. He was a wiry old, World War I veteran. These two slime balls 'done pissed him off' and 'swole up his testicles' when they held him up. He fired two shots at the robbers with his venerable Colt Peacemaker, but missed. The robber closest to him in the blue checked shirt returned fire with his H&R .32 caliber revolver. Mr. Schlisser fell to the ground, and two passersby bent over to assist. I didn't.

The two perps jumped into an avocado green, 1952 Ford Mainline sedan, which had been idling on 8th where the driver couldn't see me and I couldn't see him. They pulled out from the curb southbound, so I turned south with my red light oscillating and siren screaming like a maniacal hyena. Boggs, the getaway driver saw me now!

I radioed Dispatch about the robbery, requesting medical assistance at the liquor store, stating that I was in hot pursuit south on 8th. I described the suspect vehicle, which had an Indiana license plate, number undetermined, fleeing with three armed white male suspects.

The Chevy turned east on Market Street and then swerved north onto the 2nd Street Bridge. I called in my pursuit across the Ohio River, asking that they call the Indiana authorities.

I'm glad these yahoos didn't have a long gun, because they fired at me and/or my new cruiser at least eight times. We were cutting in and out of traffic. The getaway vehicle caused at least one collision on the bridge. The river belongs to Kentucky, so I called Dispatch and requested a unit to handle it. The bandit car and I finally arrived mostly intact on Hoosier soil. It made a sharp turn east along the river road. We were running between 60 to 65 miles per hour in a 45-mile-per-hour zone in moderate traffic on a poorly paved two-lane highway. Then the inevitable happened. An old man in a black, 1936 Hudson started to pull out from a Pure filling station, and the bandit vehicle T-boned him. They were now 'dead in the water'. I pulled up behind them and stopped.

I exited the cruiser, pulling my service revolver. I used my door as cover. A passenger from the left rear seat wearing a green work shirt exited the suspect vehicle with a Smith & Wesson .38 caliber revolver in his hand. At the same time, the perp in the blue checked shirt bailed out from the right front seat. He had a revolver too, but he couldn't get a shot at me because I was blocked from his view by the cruiser. All this movement and countermovement occurred in just a matter of seconds.

It was a no brainer - a split second reaction. It all happened by rote. My lizard brain did all the thought processing for me. I dropped green shirt with two shots in his chest.

Then I scrambled around the rear of my unit and faced off on blue checked shirt. He snapped off two rounds at me and went dry. He was out of ammo! What a shame! I returned the favor. I placed two rounds in his chest and he dropped, too, just like a sack of manure.

Up to this point, the driver must've been frozen with fear. He waited until now to exit the vehicle. He tried to carjack a motorist stuck in traffic headed westbound, but the intended victim pulled off onto the right shoulder of the road and escaped in a cloud of dust and loose gravel. Then the frantic perp spun around, pointing his Colt .32 caliber revolver at me. Terrible choice. He could have surrendered but he didn't, so I obliged him by punching his ticket with my last two rounds into his chest.

I squatted down using my cruiser as cover, and reloaded. I was about to give the driver the coup de grâce because I thought he was still alive and he definitely deserved it, but an Indiana State Trooper rolled up to the scene, so I didn't. It didn't matter. The driver was already dead. So was green shirt. Good riddance. I must say, however, I was unpleasantly shocked to see that blue checked shirt was still sucking air. This was Rufus "The Doofus" H. Dorman. Green shirt was Bradley F. Townsend. The driver was Howard K. Boggs.

ISP took over the crime scene. I followed them to their barracks when they were done. Their commander, Captain Elton B. Story, was pleased as punch that two of the three perps were now shoveling coal in Hell. He thanked and commended me. First time for anyone I knew on The Job to receive a commendation from out-of-state. I placed it in my personal file along with the others.

Mr. Schlisser, the liquor store proprietor, lived. He took a round in his upper chest, but it passed right through without doing much damage. Rufus H. Dorman got 15 years in Indiana. Then he was extradited to Kentucky, where he got 20 more, except the sentences were to run concurrently. That meant he only had to do five more years. He was released for good behavior after serving only four. Last year, he was released from Eddyville on parole. Last known address was a halfway house in Bowling Green.

Rufus H. Doorman is my fourth possible.

The last two possibles, Wilbur A. Harris and Louis D. 'Bloody Louie' Goetz were partners in dastardly crimes of perversion. My chance encounter with them was on Wednesday, October 24, 1962, just four months before I retired. I was out on patrol in the CBD when Dispatch called and said for me to meet Patrolman Emmett L. Barnett assigned to beat 104 at the callbox on the corner of 4th and Chestnut Streets. It was a Code 2 call, meaning get there quickly, with red light and siren optional. I was close, so I didn't turn on the emergency equipment. No need to alarm the public just yet.

As soon as I arrived, Emmett jumped into the cruiser. He exclaimed, "I just called in. Dispatch had just received a call of a rape in progress at 602 South Brook Street. You know who lives there?"

"No, but it doesn't matter. I guess you'll tell me anyway."

"The new City Alderman, Jake Innes. His wife phoned it in to him at work. The perps don't know she's in the house. They're raping her 16-year-old daughter, Beatrice, upstairs in her bedroom. Mrs. Innes had been next door visiting a neighbor when the perps apparently broke in. She said there's at least two. Her daughter was home sick with the flu. She called her husband, Alderman Jake, who called us. He said he didn't want this put out over the air."

"Okay. We'll park down the street and sneak in on foot. Follow my lead. This could get real ugly fast, so be prepared."

Finding a parking spot at 2 in the afternoon was not difficult. We locked up and ran to the house. Mrs. Innes was waiting by the front door. She let us in. We could hear Beatrice shrieking, and the sounds of a man shouting, "Shut the fuck up or it'll get worse!"

I told Mrs. Innes to go back to the neighbor's house, because I didn't want her to get hurt or be taken hostage. She pleaded with me not to go, but I said we were wasting time and we needed her to go for her own safety. Finally, she opened the door and left. She closed the door without making a sound.

I whispered, "Emmett, follow me as quietly as you can. The door to the bedroom opens inward to the right. You take the left side and I'll take the right. I'll go in first. Ready?"

He nodded.

The stairs had a carpeted runner so we were able to get upstairs making nary a sound. I nodded to Emmett and then slowly pushed the door wide open. Both men were naked.

One man was vigorously raping Beatrice, rutting like a savage bull on an unwilling young heifer, and the other was standing by the headboard with a knife in his right hand and stroking his erection with his left. He turned on me with a vicious snarl and I shot him in the stomach once. He fell down squealing like a pig. The other rapist looked up over his shoulder at me, his eyes filled with bloodlust and anger, but he never stopped violating the girl. I didn't hesitate. I shot him twice, high up in his back. I didn't want a through and through shot to penetrate the victim. I rushed over and ripped him off the girl, and threw him onto the hardwood floor just as hard as I could. Emmett scurried over and cuffed him behind the back. I know it hurt because he screamed out loud. Then I handed Emmett my cuffs and he did likewise to the other vile assailant, who was clutching his stomach and moaning woefully. He didn't have an erection anymore!

Beatrice was a bloody mess. They beat her severely. She was still screaming at the top of her lungs. I found her robe and helped her to put it on. I led her gently down the stairs while Emmett guarded the perps.

I found their kitchen phone and called Dispatch. I reported, "Both perps are wounded and need an ambulance. Call a separate ambulance for the female victim. Get detectives out here ASAP (as soon as possible). Call Alderman Innes and have him meet her ambulance at General Hospital ER. I'll have her mother ready to go with the ambulance in just a minute. Any questions?"

"Is the girl okay?"

"Yes and no. She's a mess. They brutally ravaged her. Make you sick to see it."

"On it, Sarge."

The cavalry arrived within minutes. The scumbags were escorted naked to the hospital, wrapped in sheets we found in the linen closet. We didn't send them until at least five minutes after Beatrice departed. We also did not perform any lifesaving measures on them, but being cockroaches, they could survive a nuclear holocaust. With 20-20 hindsight, I should have killed them both on sight. I'd killed other men for far less.

Both perps pleaded guilty to burglary, aggravated assault, and rape of a minor. They got life without parole. I didn't know if Beatrice ever did fully recover emotionally. I've never seen such trauma. I'm ashamed to say I never checked. What I saw haunted me for a long time. I read years later that she graduated from the University of Louisville with a bachelor's degree in psychology. Good for her. Maybe she was able to put this behind her.

Emmett and I received the Mayor's award for heroism and lifesaving. This time it was a plaque we could hang on our walls. This time I didn't really feel like celebrating.

Guess what. I called Eddyville today. Both scumbags escaped four months ago! I bet these are my would-be assassins. At least I hope so, because I owe them big time. Messers Harris and Goetz and I still have some unfinished business; however, in an abundance of caution, I decided to check out the other candidates first.

-12-
Running Out Leads

Thursday, April 12, 1973. I completed another tour on the night owl shift at the Kentucky State Fairgrounds. After I punched out, I spoke with my boss (Kentucky Merchant Police Company owner, Roscoe P. Walton) regarding the names my deep dive turned up. It took me six days reviewing 38 years of my police daily notebooks to develop my list of potential suspects. I no longer carry a lawman's badge, so I can't obtain criminal records on my own. I needed a sympathetic cop to help. From there, it would be easy enough for me to look up the legal documents in the Jefferson County Courthouse for additional information if that became necessary.

I rattled off my list of suspects in chronological order. Roscoe had already retired by the time my partner and I busted Wilbur A. Harris and Louis D. 'Bloody Louie' Goetz for raping Alderman Jake Innes' daughter, but Roscoe remembered the case because it generated a lot of headlines and good press for LPD. The community was outraged over what the assholes did.

He said, "You need someone in the Records Division to turn a blind eye and help you out. Lucky for you, you already know someone."

"Who?"

"Russell D. Roach. Wasn't he your partner who got shot in the Kentucky Trust Bank heist?"

"Yep. I thought he retired."

"Nope. He's Lieutenant Roach now, and he's in charge of the LPD Records Division. How's your relationship with him?"

"It's always been cordial, but I bet I haven't spoken to him in 15 years."

"Make an exhaustive wish list. Give him a call and tell him you need a favor. Then meet him for lunch and pick up the tab. Don't discuss business over the phone. Too many wagging ears. If he won't help, let me know and I'll go over his head."

"Great idea. I'll call him right now."

I called and received a cordial reception. Russ said to meet him at Mahoney's Diner on Jefferson Street at noon.

Roscoe smiled and I drove home. I studied my list. Then I showered, changed clothes, and met him like we planned.

Russ gave me a hearty hug. He said, "Long time, no see, Chet! You're looking well for a dinosaur. How the heck are you?"

We caught up on nearly 40 years of mutual history. Then he asked, "What can I do for you?"

I replied, "Russ, I've been ambushed and shot at twice in the last month. I haven't called in a report because I don't know who my assailants are or why they did it. I did make detailed reports which are on file with Roscoe over at the Fairgrounds. He suggested that I go through my old police notebooks to see if anything resonates. I did and came up with six possibles. Then I called Eddyville, to see if these mutts were still in stir. Four were released on serve-outs, and two recently escaped. What I need is a copy of the most recent mugshots Eddyville has on file on these possibles, and an opportunity to review our old police files."

"That's easy enough. Can do. Give me a list and I'll call Eddyville. Should have the photos in a week. Also, these old files are archived - in fact, some of yours are so old they might be chiseled in stone - so it may take a few days to get a clerk to locate and pull them. You can look at them in my office, but you can't remove anything. Take all the notes you want. One of these mutts wouldn't happen to be Lonnie Joseph Butts would he?"

"Yep."

"Thought so. I keep tabs on him too, for obvious reasons. He got out last year. Lives out by Iroquois Park with his sister. I heard he's got emphysema, and is finishing out his days in a wheelchair. Who else is on the list?"

I handed him my list. He perused it and said, "I heard about Harris and Goetz escaping. Those are the guys who raped the Innes girl, aren't they?"

"Yep."

"Those are probably the guys you want. I heard Jake Innes has been making life a political nightmare for the warden because of their escape. You know he's a state senator now, don't you? Pretty sure he hired a private investigator to try to locate them, not to mention all the troopers KSP has on it. He owes you big time. He lives over on Grinstead Avenue now. You might want to check with him before you initiate your own private manhunt."

"Believe me, I will. I think Harris and Goetz are my guys too, but I want to close the doors on the other four first in an abundance of caution. My home number is on that card, but

I'm listed in the telephone directory. I'm on the midnight shift over at the Fairgrounds, so you can usually reach me at home after 9 o'clock in the morning. Also, you can leave me a message at the Fairgrounds with Roscoe at anytime."

"Good deal. Tell you what. Give me a call Monday morning soon as you get off from work. I should have the files you want by then."

"Thanks, buddy. Appreciate it. I owe you."

"What are friends for? I owe you even bigger. Talk to you Monday."

I returned home and went to bed. They were having a recreational vehicle and travel trailer show at the Fairgrounds this weekend, and my presence was needed all three nights at time-and-a-half. I was happy to do it. I didn't have anything better to do - yet. Besides, I expected that I might have to take a few days off without pay.

On Monday, I reported to Russ's office. The files were waiting for me on an empty desk where a clerk normally sat, except right now Russ was down one body.

I started with the oldest file - Delbert S. Finnegan. He was released from Eddyville in 1965. He was my least likely. If he were still alive, he'd be 55. When I arrested him back in 1935, he was living with his mother, Racine Finnegan, at 2312 South 9th Street. His personal history sheet also listed a brother, Dennis R. Finnegan, who was 15 when Delbert was arrested. That would make him born around 1920, so there's a good chance he was a WWII vet, if I needed to track him down.

I checked the White Pages in the Louisville Telephone Directory for listings on Delbert, Racine, and Dennis Finnegan. Believe it or not, I hit pay dirt on Racine, at 1814

West Hill Street, telephone number 587-9124. (All the telephone numbers in the western half of Kentucky had 502 as their area code. The eastern half of the state had 606.) I called and she answered on the second ring.

"Hello."

"Is this Racine Finnegan?"

"Yes it is, but I ain't buying nothing today."

"No, ma'am. I'm not selling anything. I'm trying to get aholt of Delbert. Can I talk to him, please?"

"Who'd you say you was? Delbert's done been dead these three years now. Dumbass got hisself drunk and passed out in a vacant lot over near here and got hisself all chewed up by a passel of copperheads. Bit 57 times what the coroner said. It was terrible to behold. They say he prob'ly never felt a thang 'cause he was passed out. When they found him, he'd done shit his pants and puked all over hisself. Neighbors went out and poured gasoline on the snake hole and burnt all them sons a bitches out. Kilt 16. Nobody even knew they was there."

"Oh my gosh! I hadn't heard. Where'd you all bury him? Now that I know, I'd like to pay my respects."

"We planted him in St. Louis Cemetery over on Barret Avenue. It ain't no big marker, though. We didn't have much money and Delbert didn't have no life insurance."

"I know you all did your best. When did you say he died?"

"May 4th in 1900 and 70."

"Well, I'm so sorry to hear about this. You all take care. You hear?"

"We will. Thank you."

I wrote a note with the date detailing my call and placed

it in the file. I decided to check out the cemetery on my way home.

Next up was Lonnie Joseph Butts. I arrested him after I shot him and killed his twin brother in a bank robbery back in 1938. He had a lot of reasons for hating me. He'd be 55 now. He was released from Eddyville last year. According to the Kentucky State Penitentiary, he resides with his sister, Kimberly Tate, at 8844 New Cut Road. According to Russ, he's confined to a wheelchair with emphysema. I decided to check him out today too, on my way home.

The third file was on ex-cop Gordon T. Bertram. He's 72 years old now, released from Eddyville in 1971. He's one that really should still be doing time. Supposedly, he resides at 120 Saint Joseph Avenue in Shively. I tried looking him up in the telephone directory, but he wasn't listed. Then I called the information operator. She said this customer has an unlisted number. I reckon that means he's still alive. I decided to check him out after work tomorrow.

Moving along, I opened the file on Rufus H. Dorman. He's 53 years old now. I killed his partner and his partner's cousin, and incorrectly thought I killed him back in 1953, after they robbed a liquor store and shot the proprietor. This is a guy who probably truly wishes I were dead. I know I tried my best to make him dead. He was released on parole from Eddyville last year. The lady I spoke with there said he was living in a halfway house at 632 Turkey Trot Run, in Bowling Green, Kentucky, about 90 miles south of Louisville. That would be a day trip once I got his most recent mugshot - maybe Wednesday.

That left the two rapists who escaped from Eddyville this

past Christmas Day. I arrested them in 1962. Wilbur A. Harris was now 31 years of age. His last known address was 1511 Story Avenue, Apartment 2. His parents were listed as Derrick J. and Alma V. Harris (née Cornaby) of 836 Bardstown Road. Louis D. Goetz was 27 years old. His last known address was with his parents, Reverend Roland S. and Mrs. Barbara Kay Goetz (née Schwartz) of 1622 Newburg Road. I figured Kentucky State Senator Jake Innes would be the first person to speak with once I started down this rabbit hole.

I had learned all I could from the files. The mugshots had not come in yet. At least I did get a chance to study their mugshots when they were arrested. I returned the files to Russ and thanked him profusely. I said I would check with him tomorrow to see if the mugshots had come in.

I drove to Saint Louis Cemetery first. It took a few minutes jawboning with the octogenarian caretaker, Brother Alphonse, but he finally pointed me in the right direction. Sure enough, Delbert was buried there just like his mama said. His life had certainly been a tale of woe. It didn't sound like he ever found Jesus, but I hoped he did.

Next, I drove over to New Cut Road to check out Lonnie Joseph Butts. It was a pleasant spring day, and he was sitting out on the verandah in a rocking chair, watching the birds darting about the hanging feeder. I walked up the steps and said, "Hey, Lonnie, remember me?"

He looked terrible. I'd never have recognized him. His hair was gray and nearly all gone; his complexion was gray; and, he looked like he didn't weigh more than 120 pounds. He squinted his eyes and looked real hard through his black-framed glasses. Finally, he said, "You're the cop what shot me and my brother. What do you want, fuzz? Can't you see I'm all done for? You come to gloat?"

"No. I can see that. I'm sorry for your misfortune. I just wanted to say no hard feelings after all these years. I wish you better health."

"You didn't come to piss on my grave?"

"No, Lonnie. I think you've suffered more than enough. I just wanna let bygones be bygones."

"You said your piece, copper. Now it's time for you to get off my porch. I never want to see you again."

"As you wish. Good day."

Then I left and drove home. It was time for bed.

I called Russ on Tuesday after I got off work. He said the mugshots arrived shortly after I left yesterday. They were waiting for me in a manila envelope at the information desk in the lobby at Headquarters.

I changed clothes and went right over. I took the envelope back to my car before I opened it. The mugshot I was most interested in today was Gordon T. Bertram's. I was thankful I had it. I barely recognized him. He was bald now, nothing but fringe around his ears, and he'd picked up quite a bit of weight. He looked scruffy and shifty. I decided to stop by the Shively Police Department first. My preference was to not ruffle any police feathers, being out of my bailiwick.

It was a small department with just a few officers - maybe 20 all told, housed in a small, yellow brick building. Four marked units and one 'plain brown wrapper' were parked in front of the building. Four other automobiles, probably belonging to the cops on duty, were parked in the back lot.

The unmarked unit was a spanking new Chrysler Imperial. It was black with a red vinyl roof and a red leather interior. It was parked up next to the front door in a slot marked 'Chief'. Nice wheels. Much nicer than what LPD Chief Paul Edwards drives. Ironically, I had never rubbed elbows with SPD in all my years on The Job. I was beginning to get some bad vibes. Maybe the rumors were true. Maybe not.

Here in Shively, they still had a Desk Sergeant sitting at a massive wooden desk behind a (most likely) plexiglass window. It was reminiscent of the old days back in 1925 when I became a cop. The sergeant was elevated at least a foot higher than any walk-in citizen. This desk sergeant was about my age, heavy set, white walrus mustache, thick shock of white hair, blue eyes behind gold, wire-rimmed glasses, nickel-plated, Colt Government Model, .45 caliber semi-automatic pistol secured in a Don Hume basketweave holster and gun belt. He was wearing a large diamond ring on his right pinkie. His name tag said his last name was Kravitz. He looked like he ate well, and that he was doing very well for himself financially. Heck, his long sleeve white uniform shirt even sported French cuffs with a massive pair of gold cufflinks set with blue star sapphires. All this on sergeant's pay!

I walked up and displayed my retired LPD credentials and badge through the glass. I said, "Hello, Sergeant. My name is Chester Sinclair. I'm retired LPD. I stopped by to see if you all know an ex-con named Gordon Bertram. He got out of Eddyville a year or so ago. My understanding is he lives in some apartment over on Saint Joseph Avenue."

"Why you looking for him, bud?"

"So he does live here."

"Why you looking for him, bud?"

" I need to lay eyes on him to see if he's the person who took a shot at me a week or so ago."

"What if he ain't?"

"My question exactly. That's why I need to look at him. If it's not him, I'm adiós amigo. If it is, I'll swear out a warrant. Then we'll proceed from there."

"I think you're barking up the wrong tree, bud. It doesn't sound like him."

"Sergeant, I'm not barking up any tree. That's why I want to look at him. Would it be too much to ask for a patrolman to take me over to his digs to lay eyes on him? That's really all I'm asking. Look, I'm not trying to step on anybody's toes. I'm just asking for a little professional courtesy."

"You ain't a cop anymore, bud."

"No, and one day you won't be either. I was a patrol sergeant just like you. How would you feel if LPD gave you this same kind of third degree treatment if you needed a little professional courtesy? Come on. Whaddaya say?"

"Wait right there, bud. I gotta run this by Chief Spellman first."

"Thank you."

It was beginning to look like I'd have to do this the hard way - staking out his apartment on my own until he stepped outside.

Five minutes later Sergeant Kravitz returned with a 300-pound, cue ball bald man in a well-tailored, cobalt blue, $500 sharkskin suit, white shirt with a flashy red tie, and highly polished, brown alligator shoes. (Think Boss Hogg in the TV series, *The Dukes of Hazzard*.) He said, "I'm Chief Timothy Spellman. My understanding is you want to look at a man named Gordon Bertram to see if he's the person who took a shot at you. Is this correct?"

"Yes, Chief."

"That's it?"

"That's it."

"Moe, for Christ sakes, help this man out! Tell Woodridge to drive him over there right now so he can be on his way."

"Yes, Chief. Right away."

All 5-feet, 6-inches, 300 pounds of resplendent and sartorial Chief Timothy Spellman turned around and waddled back to his throne behind the hidden magic curtain. Sergeant Moe (*The Three Stooges?*) Kravitz got on the desk phone and made an internal call. I couldn't hear what he said. A patrolman who very much resembled Ichabod Crane (*The Legend of Sleepy Hollow*) came scrambling into the foyer like a newborn, spindly foal. He was all feet and elbows. He shook my hand vigorously and asked, "Ready to go, Sir?"

"I am."

"Let's do it."

I got into the right front seat of his nearly spotless, year-old Ford police cruiser. When we left, he said, "My name is Elvis Woodbridge. I know this dude. He's a bookie. Chief won't let us bust bookies here. You can probably guess why. I seriously doubt he's your man. Not ballsy enough, but you never know. They say he used to be on LPD. That true?"

"I'm afraid so."

"What a douche!"

He drove me directly to apartment 120, which was on the corner of the building. We walked up and Patrolman Woodbridge knocked on the door.

Bertram answered right away, like he'd been tipped off. Woodridge asked, "Mr. Bertram, you know this gentleman?"

He looked me up and down and replied, "I believe I do. Many moons ago. What do you want, Officer Sinclair?"

"Nothing, Bertram. You're not the man I'm looking for. Sorry for the inconvenience."

"Is that everything, Officer Woodbridge?"

"That's it. Have a good day, Sir."

Bertram slammed the door shut and we rode back to the police station. I'm pretty sure I embarrassed him.

Patrolman Elvis Woodridge said, "Glad to meet you, Mr. Sinclair. Hope you find your man."

"The pleasure is all mine. Thank you very much, and please extend my thanks to Chief Spellman and Sergeant Kravitz."

Then I drove home and went to bed.

On Wednesday after my shift, I told Roscoe everything I had discovered up to this point. I told him I was fixing to drive to Bowling Green to check up on Rufus H. Dorman.

Roscoe asked, "Ain't that the dude who you shot and killed his gang over in Indiana?"

"Yep."

"You'll be gone all day, then. You're taking tonight off. I'll get Bud Bailey to take your shift. Come back to work Thursday night."

"Thanks. I appreciate it."

"No problem. Mind if I give you some free advice? I don't

mean to get my nose out of joint or step on your toes."

"Roscoe, you're my closest friend and my boss. I appreciate anything you have to say which might help me."

"Okay, then. Couple of things.

"First, we're both pretty sure Dorman's not your shooter, which means while you're busy confirming it isn't him, it does not mean your assailants are on sabbatical. No doubt they're still gunning for you. So I know you Scots are tighter than a spinster's snatch, but it's high time for you to lay out a few shekels in the interest of self-preservation, as in not getting yourself killed.

"That 1950 blue Studebaker is a classic. I know you love it like vampires love blood, but right now it's time for you to park it. It stands out like a hard-on at a coronation for the Vestal Virgins. Go rent yourself a car that'll blend in anywhere, just until this matter of life and death is resolved. Get a bland Plain Jane that'll go unnoticed in any environment. Go see our old colleague, Ernie Fenwick, over at Uncle Ern's Used Car Lot. He's at Southside Drive and Strawberry Lane. He owns it. Rent something for one month. He'll give you a deal, being that you and he used to pound shoe leather on adjacent beats. If he doesn't do you right, call me from right there. He owes me."

"Okay. Done. Anything else?"

"Yes, indeed. The other issue related to your tightfistedness, is you never upgraded your hardware since you signed onto The Job back in 1925. The new .38 Specials are much more powerful than your old .38 New Colt. I understand that it's never let you down in nearly 50 years, but you ought to consider getting a more powerful pistol, or at least bringing along a shotgun or rifle just in case you get ambushed again. You know. Bring along some more firepower to your next gunfight, especially since you'll be all on your own."

"Great idea. Also done."

"Good. Make like a bird and get the flock out of here. See you Friday morning."

Roscoe was right on both accounts.

On the way home, I stopped in at the Stratton & Terstegge (S&T) Hardware store over on 4th Street. I purchased an elastic sleeve to fit over the butt of a shotgun. It had five loops to hold 12-gauge shotgun shells. I also got a tan, padded, zip-up, canvas shotgun case for a shotgun with a 26-inch barrel.

When I got home I went down in the cellar and got Papa's Sears & Roebuck, single-shot shotgun out of the cabinet. It looked great. No rust and no scuffs. Hardly ever been used since Papa wasn't a hunter. I put a light coat of oil on it. I took it and the box of 00 buckshot upstairs with me. I loaded the gun and the shot shell sleeve, and zipped up the gun in the case. Mission accomplished. Firepower duly enhanced.

I let Dink out for a little while go to potty and Bixby out to go play, which really meant to go hunting for small prey. I put food out for them both. Then I showered and changed clothes. Today I wore pleated and cuffed, cotton khaki trousers, blue and yellow argyle socks, short sleeve button-up white dress shirt, no tie, brown belt and brogans, a blue and white seersucker sport coat, and my straw Panama hat, which was turning a little yellow from age. I wore my old, reliable, .38 New Colt Police Positive revolver in a brown leather holster on my right hip, just to the right of my brown leather, six-loop, spare ammo slide. Then I called a taxi. I brought my cased shotgun and attaché case with. Cost me $1.85 including the tip, just to go to Uncle Ern's Used Car Lot.

After a brief reunion, I selected a white, 1972 Plymouth Valiant, 4-door sedan with a Slant-6, 225 cubic-inch engine, automatic transmission, AM radio, air conditioning, light blue vinyl seats, small hubcaps, blackwall tires, and only 23,000 miles. It looked like the preacher's car. Uncle Ern said it would get 20 miles per gallon. Cost me $90 for 30 days. He said if I liked it, he would sell it to me for $1,800. Actually, I thought that was a pretty good deal, especially coming from a shyster. He must really owe Roscoe big time. Maybe Ernie really liked me or he thought I would shoot him if he tried to slick me. Either way, by 10:45 I was on my way southbound to Bowling Green, Kentucky.

I arrived at the Home of the Western Kentucky University Hilltoppers at 12:30. I gassed up at a Gulf Service Station, where I got directions to the halfway house at 632 Turkey Trot Run. En route, I stumbled across Matilda's Diner, so I stopped in for a late lunch. I had a BLT, potato chips, peach pie, and a cup of black coffee. Even with a tip it only set me back $2.15.

I pulled up the driveway to the halfway house about a quarter to two. It looked like any other well-kept, brick, two-story, suburban house with white shutters and an attached, two-car garage. You'd never know it was a house full of convicted felons. The manager, a Mr. Eugene Howell, greeted me at the door. I showed him my retired LPD credentials and he let me in.

I said, "Mr. Howell, what I need to do won't take but a minute. I need to speak with Rufus H. Dorman."

"What's he done?"

"Nothing, I hope. I just need to find out if he's been in any mischief in Louisville within the last 30 days."

"I'm quite certain he hasn't. He's not allowed to leave Warren County. He doesn't have access to a car. He hasn't missed any bed checks. He gets along well with our other tenants. In fact, he's doing quite well."

"Glad to hear it. If I could just talk to him in person for about five minutes, I'm sure I can put this matter to rest. Where is he?"

"He's one if our most reliable tenants. He works 10 a.m. to 8 p.m. five days a week at the Denny's Restaurant downtown. He's a short order cook."

"Perfect. Could you call him? I'll drive over there to see him. Order a cup of coffee. He could take a short break to come over and chat with me. If he's not the man I'm looking for, and it sounds like he probably isn't, I'll be out of his hair within five minutes. Nobody but you and he needs to know anything about this. I'm not trying to get him into any trouble at work. Could you call him for me? Tell him what I'm wearing so he'll know he's talking to the right guy."

"Sure."

Mr. Howell made the call. He told Rufus I'd be there in 20 minutes. Then he gave me directions. No step for a high stepper.

I walked in and took a seat at a table next to the exterior wall with all the windows. The diner was not very busy since it was between the lunchtime and suppertime crowds. I ordered a cup of coffee and waited. Ten minutes later he came out and sat across from me.

I said, "Rufus, you remember me?"

"Vaguely. You shot me."

"You tried to shoot me."

"Yes. That was a long time ago. What do you want?"

"I want to know if you're carrying a grudge."

"Against you?"

"Yes. Against me."

"No. I was a messed up junkie back then. I'm straight now. I found the Lord. Actually, He found me. I apologize for my bad behavior in the past. I'm thankful I didn't shoot you or I'd still be in prison, assuming I wasn't already executed after years of worrying about it on Death Row. I bear no animosity towards you."

"And I bear none against you. Thanks for talking with me. Go with God."

"Go with God."

I drove back to Louisville. I picked up a pizza from Mr. Gatti's Pizza Parlor and arrived home about 4 o'clock. I spent some quality time with Dink and Bixby. I smoked a cigar and sipped on some Old Dr. Crow. Dink played fetch and Bixby caught a blue-tail lizard. Apparently the lizard was quite tasty. Then I watched a little television. I thought hard about my situation. Just like Roscoe, I had known my investigation would lead me back to Wilbur A. Harris and Louis D. Goetz. I thought now I would have some help finding them. At least I hoped so, because I could never rest in peace unless they were both dead or back in prison. It mattered not to me which.

"That ain't no way to go." - Brooks & Dunn

-13-
Getting Down to Brass Tacks

Friday morning after work, Roscoe and I had our usual little tête-à-tête. First thing he wanted to know is if I were the one driving the white Valiant parked out back. All I said was, "It's the new me. Mr. Blending In, a/k/a Mr. Anonymous. It seems to be working, too. Now folks don't stare at me when they see me coming, feeling sorry for me that I can't afford a newer car. Now they just look at me rolling around in this granny car and mutter to themselves, "Look at that poor stiff. He probably hasn't been laid since Harry Truman was President."

"I think it suits you just fine, buddy boy. You've always been a half-bubble off center when it comes to automobiles. Face it, Chet. You're basically a pedestrian. Even the Army thought so, making you straight-leg infantry. Even took your division's wheels away from them, probably just because of you. Made you walk to war, just like the Roman Legions. I assume now you're ready to get down to nut cutting."

"I am. Thing is, I wonder how it is nobody's popped a cap at me since March 16th. This is April 20th. The first encounter was February 22nd. That was two months ago. Nada in more'n a month. Was I hallucinating?"

"You sound like you wanna be dead."

"I sound like I'm starting to have doubts about my own sanity. I haven't even felt the hair on the back of my neck stand up, even when I did get shot at. I haven't noticed anyone tailing me. My house is unmolested. If Harris and Goetz want me dead after 10 years, how's come they gave up so easily? I don't get it."

"Who knows? By the way, Jake Innes's law office is on the 8th floor of the Heyburn Building at 4th and Broadway. Go home and get cleaned up and go see him. See what he says before you blow this off as fanciful thinking."

That's exactly what I did. Fortunately, Senator Innes had time to visit with me. He asked, "How may I be of assistance, Mr. Sinclair?"

"Sir, you probably don't remember me. I'm retired now, but I'm the policeman who shot and arrested both Wilbur A. Harris and Louis D. Goetz."

"I thought you looked familiar. Of course! My whole family is indebted to you, Sir.

"I guess by now you've heard those scoundrels somehow managed to escape from Eddyville. Kentucky State Police (KSP) has a whole task force looking for them. Ha! That's a joke! I get weekly updates, but so far, they haven't been able locate them. They couldn't find a Jew in Tel Aviv."

"That's what I heard, and that's why I'm here.

"Since I retired, I've been employed by the Kentucky State Fairgrounds as a security officer on the midnight shift. While I was at work on February 22nd, an unknown white male who managed to secrete himself inside the building after hours, took a shot at me. He was wearing a bandanna over his face. He took me by surprise. After he fired, I chased him into the back parking lot, but he managed to get away. I looked everywhere but couldn't find him.

"I wrote it off as an entrant with a display in the trade

show who I may have startled as he was planning to sabotage the display of a competitor. I couldn't come up with any other scenario. I looked diligently, but couldn't find a spent projectile. He shot at me with a blue steel revolver, so he didn't leave a shell casing. I'd hazard a guess he used a .38.

"Then on March 16th, as I was returning to my car at the A&P at 6th and Hill, an unknown party shot at me with a .30 caliber rifle. I know, because I recovered the slug. Anyway, I didn't see who did it, but I believe the assailant sped off in a late model black sedan, maybe a Ford, and I think someone else was doing the driving.

"I have no information related to whom shot at me either time, or why, but I certainly believe both incidents were connected. To my knowledge, I had no enemies up until these two incidents.

"I did an exhaustive search of all my police notebooks looking for possible shooters, and came up with two names - Wilbur A. Harris and Louis D. Goetz. That was before I realized they had escaped from prison. Bottom line is, I now have a dog in the fight with respect to finding them. Sir, would you help me? I seriously doubt KSP would welcome my interest."

"Did you file a report regarding these incidents with LPD?"

"No. what I did was file reports with my boss, Roscoe P. Walton, owner of the Kentucky Merchant Police Company. He's a retired LPD lieutenant, and he has the security contract for the Kentucky State Fairgrounds. I've been there nearly ten years. I retired from LPD as a sergeant after 38 years. Other than the spent projectile recovered at A&P, I have no evidence. I can tell you with certainty from many years of experience, neither of these attempted murders would gain any traction in Homicide, unless I could tie them all together with a nice little bow."

"Sadly, I believe you're right.

"This is what I know about Harris and Goetz. They escaped from Eddyville by bribing a correction officer on the midnight shift. When he realized he was about to be arrested, he committed suicide by carbon monoxide poisoning in his garage. He was divorced with two kids, and way behind in his support payments with virtually no way to catch up. I'm certainly not excusing him, but at least I understand his motive.

"KSP's Fugitive Felon Squad is assigned to track down Harris and Goetz. The team of six detectives - and I use that term loosely - is headed up by Sergeant Alvin T. Samples out of Frankfort. It's completely composed of rural officers, of whom I have no doubt are excellent in their element; however, they don't know diddly squat about working fugitives in an urban area. Also, this case is just one of dozens they're currently working, so they're performing lip service to me because they have to. They'd prefer it if I just went away, but that's not going to happen. At least that's my opinion. Just like the FBI, KSP thinks they're better than local cops. In fact, to that point, to the best of my knowledge, they have yet to coordinate with LPD or Jefferson County. Imagine that.

"They report to me once a week because of my official position in Kentucky state government. If I didn't have a modicum of political clout, they'd blow me off. All they do is inform me of their non-progress. All they've managed to determine so far, is that neither suspect has been in touch with his folks. Based upon my own endeavors, I'm inclined to believe it.

"Do you know Eliot R. Quick? He's a retired LPD auto theft detective."

"I know who he is. I never had any cases with him."

"He's a licensed private investigator. Pretty reputable, too. I hired him to see what he could dig up on Horrid Harris and Gruesome Goetz after they broke out of prison. He provided me with a pretty comprehensive dossier on both perps and their families, and he did it in just three days, so that's all he charged me for. He's an honest professional.

"Harris's father, Derrick, is a State Farm insurance agent. Makes a good living.

"Son Wilbur is a bad egg. He was in so much trouble throughout his life, the family was finally compelled to disown and disinherit him. They never even came to see him in the hospital, or jail, or prison from the point you arrested him. They're embarrassed of him and have avoided all contact.

"Wilbur's got an older brother, Phillip, who's a junior partner with his dad at State Farm. I've spoken with both Derrick and his wife, Alma. They're frightened to death of Wilbur. They've purchased an expensive alarm system for their home and business, and Derrick doesn't go anywhere without a gun anymore. Both said they would let me know if Wilbur reached out to them. It's been awhile, so I'll check in with Derrick later on today.

"Goetz's father, Roland, is a Lutheran minister. I've spoken with him and his wife, Barbara Kay. They're both horrified of the person Louis has become. They tried to be supportive of him initially, but he was unrepentant, and never gave up his evil ways. Before he evolved into becoming a rapist, he was a serial window peeper. He got caught masturbating outside their neighbors' houses twice. He even tried to rape his sister when she was 14, but she hit him with a lamp and got away. That was the last straw. His folks finally threw up their hands and gave him the boot. Roland even told me that in the interest of public safety, Louis belongs in prison for the rest of his life.

"Bottom line is, I very much doubt Harris or Goetz have been in contact with their folks since they've been on the lam.

"Are you a PI, Mr. Sinclair?"

"No, Sir. All I am is a licensed security officer."

"When you leave my office today, march yourself over to the courthouse and get a PI license. You're retired LPD so all you gotta do is fill out the application and pay $25.00 for the first year's license fee. Then I will retain you to work on this case for one dollar a year. Even give you a receipt. You and I will work this case together. Don't bother calling KSP. They'll stonewall you and be miffed with me for hiring you.

"The black getaway car is the first real lead in this case so far. Nobody but you and I know about it. Check with your pals in auto theft and see what's been reported stolen in Louisville and Jefferson County since Christmas. Let's try that angle first. I feel pretty darn certain that Harris and Goetz returned to Louisville. It's all they know. Besides that, it sounds like they both have a real vendetta against you. This seems to be what motivates them. I guarantee they're right here in our own backyard.

"It also wouldn't hurt to check if any recent rapes have a

suspect which matches either of their descriptions, but do the stolen cars first.

"Chester, if you want these perps behind bars, it'll be up to you and me. No one else will do it. Any reservations? It'll be a lot of work."

"No, Sir."

"Call me Monday morning when you get off work."

"Roger that."

"I scooted on over to the Jefferson County Courthouse and obtained an occupational license to be a private investigator. No heavy lifting. I wondered why I never thought of that before. Then I went to LPD Headquarters up on the 2nd floor to the Detective Bureau (DB). I got lucky. Detective Lieutenant Beau Ames was up front. I knew him from back in the day when he walked Beat 10 next to me on Beat 7.

He said, "Chester, how the heck are you? Get your rear end inside here and have a cuppa joe with me."

He unlatched the half-door and let me in. We drank coffee. Beau lit up a Lucky Strike. I refreshed my dip of Copenhagen smokeless tobacco. We took a merry stroll down Memory Lane. Finally he asked, "What's on your mind, Chet?"

"You remember that case about ten years ago when Emmett Barnett and I busted those two scumbags who were raping Alderman Jake Innes's daughter?"

"Don't you mean Senator Jake Innes?"

"Yeah, but that was back before Jake made senator."

"Just breaking your stones, Chet. Checking to see if you're up to speed on current affairs."

"Oh, I am. I just came from Jake's office. You remember that case?"

"You mean the case where you and Emmett were awarded everything but the key to the city? You all were our local Batman and Robin. Who could forget that? All you had to do was say the word and you'd have made lieutenant overnight."

"Beau, you know me better than that. I was a great patrol sergeant, but I would have been a horrible lieutenant. Besides, I had my eyes set on retiring by then."

"If you say so. What about that case?"

"Both Wilbur Harris and Louis Goetz escaped from Eddyville on Christmas Day. Two times since then someone's taken a pot shot at me, but fortunately they missed. I'm pretty sure it's them. KSP's Fugitive Felon Squad has been assigned to track 'em down and end their lawless ways, but it's been nearly five months. I'm sure you can correctly guess their progress."

"Yep. If it's not a DWI, vehicular homicide, high speed driving, or hit-and-run, they're completely out of their league."

"Bingo. Pretty much. I told you I got my PI license, and this is why. Senator Jake Innes retained me to track Harris and Goetz down before they kill me or I die of old age. I have one slim lead and that's why I'm here."

"Did you report these two attempted murders to Homicide?"

"Nope. Beau, would you want to take on a case like this with virtually no clues when you already have a double caseload?"

"Point well taken. That really means 'You're a good man, Charlie Brown.' What do you need from me?"

"Simple. The second time I was shot at, the shooter escaped in a late model black sedan. I'd like to look at the list of cars stolen locally since Christmas. Maybe I'll get a lead."

"That's a long shot, buddy. Even if you ID the car, it doesn't mean Harris or Goetz stole it, and even if they did, they've probably already ditched it."

"Right you are. Did you forget my real job is working midnights for Roscoe Walton over at the Fairgrounds? I told you Chloe passed away three years ago. I've got the time. What else am I going to do? Sit on my hands until they try to pop me again?"

"All salient points. I'll get you the list you want going back to December 25th. It will include the dates and times, names, addresses, and telephone numbers of all the victims, plus the site of the theft. Don't let anyone know I gave this to you. Destroy it after you're done. Capice?"

"Capice."

"Check at the Information Desk tomorrow. It'll be waiting for you in a plain brown envelope. Don't forget to tell Senator Innes I stuck my neck out for you. I might need a favor from him someday."

"Done. Thanks, Beau."

"Find the bastards, Chet, before they find you again."

"On it."

It was noon. I went home and slept like a baby, but not before checking the premises thoroughly for signs of an unwanted visitor. There were none. I would be busy, working the weekend for the Kentucky-Indiana Gun & Knife Show, all overtime. Night. Night.

-14-
Grinding It Out

It took me a long time to get to the place I was now, regarding my likely assassin(s). From the point that they tried to kill me at the A&P, I've watched my back trail, set up tells around my house, and done everything I could think of to identify and track them down. I haven't even seen or smelled so much as a wisp of smoke.

Saturday night between tours around the exhibit halls, I scoured the list of stolen cars in Jefferson County since Christmas day. Altogether, there were 63. There were ten black, late model sedans, plus two which were navy blue. Eight of the cars were compacts, including a Falcon, two Corvairs, a Dart, Valiant, two Mustangs, and a Camaro. That left four - one blue Impala, two black Galaxies, and one black Coupe de Ville. The auto I saw was clearly not a Caddy, so that left me with three possibles.

Now what? When I got off from work, I would make a trip to the homes of those three victims to see if they had any information which might help me. In the interim, I looked at the theft sites to see if I could pick up any patterns. Ditto regarding approximate times of the thefts. It didn't help. Nearly all the thefts occurred at night, and there didn't seem to be a particular neighborhood or area of town which was particularly hard hit.

This was beginning to look like an exercise in futility, just like Beau said. I was running out of ideas. I knew trying to get

Sex Crimes to let me look at their records would be a next to impossible accomplishment. LPD is extra sensitive when it comes to identifying victims of sexual assault, and you can understand why. At the same time, active rapists have to be getting their jollies somewhere. For degenerates like Harris and Goetz, that meant inflicting pain and terror. The most likely victims would be paid prostitutes who got more than they bargained for. I might get some help on that angle from the Vice Squad. They would most likely know the names of recently brutalized working girls.

I wrote down the three addresses I needed to visit. I knew where two were located. I had to look up the third one from a commercial *Louisville Book Map*.

Roscoe was up to his ears in alligators when I punched out, so I didn't even say goodbye. I'd been driving the Valiant for several days now. I thought I was invisible and anonymous, but I picked up a tail on my way out of the parking lot. It wasn't a black sedan, either. It was a pale blue, six or eight-year old Chevy G-10 workman's van with two white males. I couldn't make out their faces. My adrenaline started pumping. How did I want to work this?

I decided to pretend I didn't notice them and drive towards home. I made an unnecessary right turn at the last minute just to see if the van would follow. It did. I noticed a Circle K convenience store I'd never stopped at before, but today I did. I was only in long enough to purchase a tin of Copenhagen. When I came out, I caught the van across the street from the corner of my eye. It was backed in, so I couldn't see a plate. It probably didn't matter anyway. The van was probably stolen.

Now what? Do I lead them back to my house? Hell, my address and telephone number were listed in the Bell South Telephone Directory! I'd be a fool to think they didn't already know where I lived. I took my time, but drove on home. They dropped off when I turned onto Floyd. I went inside and watched through the front window. A few minutes later, the van passed by.

This was really frustrating. I had been unable to see their faces clearly. All I could swear to is that they were both white males without facial hair between 30 and 40 years of age. I checked the stolen vehicle list and the van wasn't on it. It was old enough that they probably bought it from someone with a sign in the windshield for less than $500.

Both Dink and Bixby wanted to go out, so I let them out the back door. I pulled Papa's shotgun out of it's case. I double-checked it due to my anal retentiveness. Yep. It was still loaded. I fixed myself a breakfast of orange juice, patty sausage, grits, and toast with grape jelly. No caffeine. I needed to sleep and I needed to keep watch. I compromised. I slept in my recliner in the parlor with the shotgun across my lap. I didn't even take off my shoes. It would be up to Dink and Bixby to stand watch.

I awoke with a start. I didn't know why. I hadn't heard anything. It was dark outside. I checked my watch. It was 7:30. Dink was asleep at my feet and Bixby was asleep on the front windowsill. I didn't know I was that tired. I finally roused myself and checked the house and yard carefully. No one there. No van parked down the street. If my neighbors had seen me walking around my yard with a shotgun they would have thought I'd come unhinged.

I took a shower and got cleaned up. I put a fresh coat of polish on my shoes. I cleaned my .38. Then I put on a clean uniform and girded up. I fed the home security force, and let them go back outside while I cooked my supper. More sausage, Aunt Jemima pancakes, real maple syrup, a banana, and a fresh pot of black coffee - half for now and half to fill my old Stanley thermos. I made my lunch consisting of two bologna and mustard sandwiches, some Charley's potato chips, two oatmeal cookies, and an apple. I was basically ready for work by 10 o'clock, but it was too early. What to do? I was full of indecision.

Tonight I left a small lamp on in the parlor and turned on both the front and back porch lights. I gave the security force their treats. I locked up and left. I took the cased shotgun with me. Then I drove down the street and parked between two panel vans in the lot belonging to Floyd Street Plumbing. I turned off the lights and watched. At 11:30, after having seen no criminal activity, I drove to work. It was a long, slow night. I had been poised for danger, but none came my way.

After work, I went home and cleaned up. I spent more quality time with Dink and Bixby. Then I left and ate a quick breakfast at McDonalds before going to church. After church, I started checking on the three stolen cars. All three victims had been reimbursed by their insurance companies. The blue Impala had been recovered by the Indianapolis Police Department, and turned over to the insurance company. The 1971 black Galaxie had been found burned out in the West End. The 1972 black Galaxie owned by Mr. and Mrs. Ernst Schultz, at 1710 Taylorsville Road had never been recovered. I began to think that was the car used in the getaway after they shot at me at the A&P, but I had no way of knowing for sure. If it were, they had probably switched out the license plate from a similar car. Nevertheless, I still had the original license plate number. I had done all I could do until after I checked in with Jake Monday morning.

Monday, April 23rd. I'd been spinning my wheels for two weeks. I told Roscoe about the blue van which tailed me from work Saturday morning. All he said was, "At least now you know you weren't hallucinating." I told him I needed a couple of days off. He agreed, and said he would see me Thursday morning after my shift.

I called Jake and gave him an update. I told him I was out of leads, and the reservations I had about asking for sexual assault cases from the Sex Crimes unit. He agreed.

He said the Harris and Goetz families had not been contacted by their sons.

I told him my idea to check with the Vice Squad on prostitutes who had been abused by their johns. He liked the idea. He said maybe one of them had seen the driver of either of the suspect vehicles. I said I would try to find out.

I went back to LPD. I went to the Vice Squad office. Sergeant Victor Gonzales was the only one there. I knew him casually from back in the day when I regularly attended the Fraternal Order of Police (FOP) meetings at Lodge 6. He was one of the elected officers. His nickname was Gonzo. He looked up when I knocked on the doorframe and walked in.

I said, "Gonzo. Remember me? Chet Sinclair. It's been a long time."

"You were a patrol sergeant, right? Crazy bastard who preferred a walking beat in the CBD?"

"Guilty as charged. Got a minute? I need to run something by you."

"Geez, I hope you're not here looking for a working girl who's disappeared. That seems to be the only reason people ever want to see me anymore."

"Nope."

"Well come on in, anyway. Shut the door. Grab a seat and a cup of joe."

I did.

He asked, "How have you been? I haven't seen you around."

"Well, the short version is, I retired 10 years ago. I took a job working for Roscoe Walton at the Fairgrounds on midnight shift. My wife, Chloe, died three years ago. Now it's just the dog and cat and me in the same house I grew up in over on South Floyd. What about yourself?"

"Been in Vice six years now. I have 28 years in, so I hope to retire in two more. Got one kid who's career Army. He's got nine years, Infantry Branch, 82nd Airborne Division, stationed at Fort Bragg, North Carolina. Daughter's a nurse at Baptist Hospital. She's got two kids. Wife and I will celebrate 26 years of marriage in another month.

"I'm sorry to hear about your wife. You had a son killed in action in Korea didn't you?"

"Yes. Arnold. He was Infantry too, as was I. I'm humbled you remembered."

"You never forget things like that when it happens to someone you know. I worry about my own son. Infantry's a dangerous job. I was in the Navy during the war, a gunner's mate on a heavy cruiser. We had our moments, but it wasn't like the guys in the Army or Marines on the front line.

"What brings you in today?"

I synopsized my two episodes of being shot at, and what I'd done so far to find the shooters. I told him my investigation was a joint effort with Senator Jake Innes. Then I explained my thoughts that Harris and Goetz, being serial rapists, had probably roughed up some working girls, and maybe his guys had heard something about it, not knowing Harris and Goetz were prison escapees serving life sentences. I also mentioned that Sex Crimes probably had seen some of their handiwork too, but I knew they would never share with me.

He replied, "I hadn't heard they escaped. I remember them raping Jake's daughter, and that you were the one who caught them. I'm on board with you and Jake 100%.

"Tell you what. I'll pull their mugshots and have some copies made. Spread 'em around to my detectives. I have one, Melinda Bates, who's got a really good rapport with the working girls. If anyone can get them to talk, it's her. Give me a few days. Call me Thursday if I haven't called you first. In the meantime, you better cover your 6 (military term for back, derived from 6 o'clock being at the rear of 12 o'clock).

"Oh yeah, I'll also talk to Sergeant Dennis Beaumont over in Sex Crimes. He may share some information with me. Harris and Goetz are probably a couple of his unknown suspects. Your information may help solve some of his active cases. Any one of us would love to be the one to permanently end their revolting crime spree. We all have wives and sisters and daughters. I'll be in touch."

"Thanks a million. I wish everyone good luck. Bye."

I stopped by Jake's office on my way home. For now, I had played out my string. Besides checking my 6, all I could do was wait, or so I thought. Jake thought otherwise. Since I had a couple of days off, he recommended I go the *Courier Journal's* morgue and scour for articles of recent rapes. He knew victim names wouldn't be included, but oftentimes the street and block number of crimes are reported. What else did I have to do? Off I went.

All the newspapers were stored on microfiche. I sat at a table, and went through each newspaper since Christmas, page by page, on a black and white TV screen. I wrote down the date and location of all the rapes which had any coverage. This was tedious work. I did all I could do by 3 o'clock. I was up to February 10th. I had found 34 listings by then, although with so much information redacted, I really couldn't tell if any of these were of interest. I would try to finish up by tomorrow.

I kept my beady bulbs busy scanning for the blue van or the black Galaxie on the way home. Nada. I stopped at the A&P for groceries - this time three paper bags full, not to mention a six-pack of RC Colas. I also stopped by Morgan's Liquor Store for a fifth of Old Dr. Crow. I arrived home safely, no hostiles on my horizon. The security team was ecstatic when I walked in. I got fussed at for being late, and I sorely deserved it.

Soon as I put the perishables in the fridge, I sat out back and watched my furry children play. I indulged with one of my Punch Churchill Maduro cigars and a taste or two of Old Dr. Crow on the rocks. I might have been getting mellow, but security was ever-most present on my mind. The 12-gauge was leaning in the corner to my right, and my .38 was where it always was - somewhere on my waist.

After Happy Hour, I went back inside and made supper. Tonight it was Swiss steak and brown gravy, corn on the cob, carrots and celery sticks, Italian bread with butter, and iced tea. Dessert was a slice of store-bought cherry pie.

After cleaning up the kitchen, Dink and Bixby and I watched television. In those days we only had two choices on my black-and-white boob tube - CBS and NBC. Tonight it was Barnaby Jones followed by a rerun of Paladin, while I sipped on some more bourbon. I shut it off before the news. Dink went out to sprinkle the grass and then we all went to bed.

Was today a good day or bad? I decided it was good, though it wasn't particularly gratifying.

Tomorrow would be a new day.

-15-
A New Day

I woke up early. It was about 6:30. I turned on the percolator which I had set up the evening before. The security team went outside. I wasn't looking forward to another day at the *Courier Journal* morgue. There was a reason my entire police career was in patrol, most of it on foot patrol. I loved the interface I had with the public. I loved the spontaneity of patrol. What I didn't much care for was the grind of investigations. Not my cuppa tea pouring over files like I had been doing at the morgue. I liked being in uniform. I still do. Nevertheless, that was my fate today, or so I thought.

I fixed two boiled eggs, patty sausage, grits, toast, and orange juice for breakfast. I drank four cups of black coffee. I played a little fetch with Dink. Then I cleaned up. It was 8:45 when I got ready to go.

I was fixing to step out the front door when I saw THE blue van pull part way up my drive, which is about eight feet to the right of my house looking out the front door. Now that I could see the front end, I could tell it was a '65 model in good repair. Papa's shotgun was leaning up against the wall by the front door, so I picked it up and cocked it. When I opened the door, the van started to back up.

The bushes in front of my house are all low, as in maybe two feet tall. They're spaced almost a foot apart. I hate bushes, but these were a concession to Chloe. Snakes and leaves and blowing trash like to collect under bushes. They're difficult to mow under. Sometimes yellow-jackets nest in the ground under them. Bushes have a tendency to die under my lackadaisical care. That's why I hate them. Bushes serve no useful purpose for me. Today, my penchant against bushes largely played a roll in saving my life.

My front door opens in to the left and my screen door opens out to the right as you're exiting. As I was stepping out onto the porch, which is only eight inches high, I detected a shadow or movement to my left. I wasn't paying attention to my footing, and I slipped and fell forward, but didn't fall down. Truthfully I was focused on the van. An assassin came from around the left side of my house, aiming a rifle at me. I recognized it in a flash. It was a Marlin Model 336, .30-30 caliber, lever action carbine. He fired just as I fell forward, and fortunately for me his shot missed.

I could see him clearly from that distance since he had no cover. I fired at him center of mass. The nine .33 caliber balls in that 12-gauge shell only had an eight-inch spread from that distance, and I blew his black heart out his back in small meaty pieces. He fell to the ground with a thump. Although I was wearing my .38, instead of pulling it, I elected to put another shell in Papa's shotgun. I wanted the extra lethality.

I pointed it at the front windshield of the van, and put nine holes in the windshield as it was backing out. This was an option available to me, because the van had been forced to stop due to a passing motorist. The spread was much greater at that distance, and I'm not sure if I hit the driver, but hit or not, he managed to get away. I was too far away to read the license plate number, but for damn sure, I'd recognize that van if I ever saw it again.

My next-door neighbor, Herb Allison, came running over

to help. He was carrying the Army Colt .45 he liberated from a dead Army captain on the beaches of Normandy. He stopped short when he saw what all was missing from Louis Goetz. He said, "Dern, Chet! That scoundrel tried to ambush you! You blowed a hole through his chest big enough to put your fist through. His heart's scattered into a dozen pieces. Know who he is?"

"I sure do. It's Louis D. Goetz. The driver of the blue van is Wilbur A. Harris. They escaped from Eddyville. I arrested them for aggravated rape ten years ago. They both were serving life sentences without parole. Looks like Louis just completed his and won't have to go back."

"Hey! I told Amy (his wife) to call the cops. They should be on their way."

"Could you stand guard for a minute? I need to make a call."

"You bet! I ain't going nowhere. The other'n may double back on you. If he does I'll fix his little red wagon."

"Thanks. Be back in a jiffy."

I called Jake at his office. I told him what happened in a nutshell. He said he was on his way and not to make any statements until he arrived. I figured he'd need ten minutes to get here coming from his office. I took off my gun and put it in my top dresser drawer. I knew I'd be taking a ride downtown, and I didn't want it confiscated.

The beat car was pulling into the drive when I went back outside. My shotgun was leaning in the corner of the porch - empty. I walked out to greet the officers. I knew the driver, Patrolman Leon Bagby. Once upon a time he was on my platoon. I didn't know the younger one. He was a rookie. He introduced himself as Patrolman Cecil Whitaker.

Leon said, "Doggone, Sarge. Looks like you had a little trouble. Who's your friend?"

"That's my neighbor, Herb Allison. He ran over once he heard the shots to see if he could help."

"Give me just a sec to cancel the other unit. I'll get homicide on the way."

Jake rolled up just as Leon was getting back out of the cruiser.

Leon asked, "Senator Innes, what brings you here?"

"Hi, Officer. I'm Chet's legal counsel."

"Glad to see you, Sir, but from what I can tell, Chet don't need no counsel."

"I agree. I'm just here in an abundance of caution. Mind if I take him aside for a minute?"

"No, Sir. Have at it."

We chatted for about 10 minutes. I went over everything which had transpired, chapter and verse. He asked, "You okay?"

I replied, "You bet. This isn't my first time killing a villain. I'm fine, even peachy."

A bevy of homicide dicks and crime scene investigators (CSI) showed up. So did Detective Lieutenant Beau Ames. He greeted me and Jake warmly. Then he said, "Your fears were certainly warranted, Chet. I'm just thankful it came out this way."

"Me, too, but you know Wilbur Harris isn't going to give up this easy. It was him driving the blue van."

"We've got a BOLO (Be on the Lookout) out. Hopefully a patrol car will find it."

It took the better part of two hours for CSI to complete their investigation. Then I got into Jake's Cadillac and we all went downtown. On the way down he said, "I can see, you've still got a lot of friends on the job. You want your shotgun back?"

"I most certainly do. Heck yeah. It was my papa's."

"I'll make sure you get it. I'm sorry this had to happen, but thanks for erasing Gruesome Goetz from the gene pool. He was a nasty piece of work."

"You're very welcome. Wish I had killed him ten years ago. Ditto re Harris. I hope at least of one of my buckshot got him good, like in an artery. I couldn't tell for sure if he was hit."

We spent the better part of two hours in Homicide. I wrote out my official statement. Jake reviewed it and said, "I could successfully defend this statement in any court of the land."

I had called Roscoe and he brought the reports I had written regarding the two attacks made against me, plus the spent .30 caliber projectile. Detective Ralph Bradshaw included them in the official file. He said Forensics would try to match the projectile to the Marlin.

Detective Alvin Winters located a police report from December 29th, which documented a burglary from Gates Ace Hardware on 3rd Street. That's where the Marlin rifle and a Ruger Security Six, .38 Special caliber revolver were stolen, along with several boxes of ammunition, a hunting knife, and various miscellaneous items, to include a pair of Bushnell binoculars. He said, "Well, I bet I can guess what revolver Wilbur Harris is carrying. To bad you couldn't find that other spent round (at the fairgrounds)."

While I was there, Lieutenant Beau Ames reported that Patrol had located the blue van. It was abandoned in an alley near Saint James Court. There was blood, not a lot, on the back of the driver's seat. They were towing it to the police garage for a full forensics examination. It was beginning to look like at least one buckshot may have hit pay dirt.

Beau said, "Chet, you got the entire department energized. We'll find this bastard. I'd detail someone to keep watch at your house, but you know we don't have the assets. However, Patrol has been instructed to make several drive-bys past your house on each shift, at least until we get Harris."

"Thanks, Beau. I couldn't ask for anymore than that."

"Keep a watchful eye out. You know now Harris is determined more than ever to rub you out. Alvin will return your shotgun, and you can be on your way. Best of luck. If you need anything, don't hesitate to call, night or day."

"Thanks. Will do."

Then Jake and Roscoe and I hustled over to the Blue Boar for lunch.

When I returned home, I cleaned the shotgun and replaced the two shells I had fired. That was pretty much the sum total for that day except for hanging out with the security team, burning another cigar, and nursing a few tastes of Old Dr. Crow. I wasn't shot, but in a manner of speaking, I was 'shot in the ass'. I didn't feel like doing anything. Life or death situations have a way of prompting a man to take his own tally. Try to figure out if his life was on the plus or minus side of the ledger. I decided mine was on the plus, but it highlighted just how much I missed Chloe and Arnie. I really felt all alone. Good thing I had the furry security team.

I went back to work Wednesday night. Everything was same-old, same-old, except it wasn't. I wished that I knew where Harris lay his rotten head at night, except I didn't. I do know he never went to a hospital for treatment. Homicide had put all of them on notice to call if he did. Besides, they already knew the law required them to report gunshot injuries. No such luck. I'm of Scottish descent, but sometimes it seemed like I was cursed with the opposite version of the luck of the Irish. I knew that wasn't really true. I was lucky to be alive. I apologized to God.

Monday morning after work, April 30th to be exact, I received a call from Gonzo at Vice. He asked me to stop by. His call alone got my juices flowing. I showered and changed clothes and hurried down to see him.

Gonzo said, "I wish I would have gotten this information before your encounter with Harris and Goetz, but I didn't. Maybe it's just as well. You already terminated half of the problem.

"Melinda found three working girls who wish they'd never seen either one of these butt wipes. Their street names are Trixie, Queenie, and Sapphire. Trixie's white and the other two are black. All three work East Market Street from 1st to 5th. Trixie's a freelancer but the other two worked for a pimp named Tyrone Washington. They don't anymore.

"You want the Cliff Notes version, or the unsanitized version? It's pretty gruesome, especially if you have daughters."

"Tell me everything you know. I despise these reprobates from the depths of my soul for all the people they've wounded or killed and savagely debased, not least of which is myself. Even Jesus would have to hold his nose if either of them repented and came to him for salvation."

"You're right about that. Okay. Here goes, but I warned you. Tell me if you change your mind, because this will make you sick to your stomach. It does me, and I work Vice. I'm still not immune from it yet.

"Trixie was first, sometime around New Years. She has a little substance problem, so she couldn't remember for sure about the date. By the way, all three girls identified Harris and Goetz from their mugshots.

"When Trixie met them, they were in a black sedan, type unknown. They wanted to know if she'd take a double. She said she would for double the price, which was $20 bucks each for 30 minutes total. Harris gave her $20 up front, and she got in the car.

"She led them back to her crib, which is a backroom apartment in the rear of a dive called the Bucket of Blood Saloon farther down on Market. It's at 8th, I think. They all went inside.

"Trixie started stripping, but before she was completely naked, she asked for the other $20. Goetz ponied up, and asked if she would do bondage. She said yes, for another $20 each, so they both ponied up again. She reminded them that all they had paid for was 30 minutes. Harris said that was all they needed.

"Goetz tied her wrists to the head posts. Then both guys got naked. Harris mounted her first. When he was done, Goetz mounted her, only he took her anally, which wasn't part of the agreement. That costs extra. She started screaming and kicking and trying to resist, and that's when he hit her hard in the face twice. He told her to shut up and hold on because he hadn't had a woman in a long time and he was planning to knock the bottom out if it.

"He reamed her out for a long time. Then he got off and Harris did her anally, too. Goetz told her to do him orally while Harris was doing her anally. She bit his penis hard, drawing blood, and he beat the living daylights out of her while Harris continued banging her backdoor.

"He got done, and told her to lick him off. This time she complied. Then Goetz climbed back on and did her vaginally. He got done and told her to lick him off. She did. Then Harris did her again anally. Same thing. He made her lick him off. Goetz did her vaginally one more time. Then they washed off in the sink. The perps got dressed. They left without untying her. She said she believes they did her for nearly two hours.

"It took her several hours to get loose. She cleaned up as best she could. Then she got a friend to take her to General Hospital. She had a broken nose, two black eyes, rope burns on both wrists, a swollen anus, and a seriously bruised vagina. The ER nurse tried to get her to make a police report, but she said she didn't know who her assailants were, and that all she wanted to do was go home.

"She made $80 that night, but took a terrible beating, and was laid up for two weeks recovering. The only income she made during that time was by performing oral sex. That's when it occurred to her to walk down to Male High School just before classes let out. Quite a few boys have cars these days, so she set up shop in the back seat of a car whichever boy was willing to let her use. The car owner got a freebee and the others paid $10 bucks each. She said she made over a hundred bucks a day each time she went there. She also said high school boys were so horny they got off in just two or three minutes. Some even paid to come back for seconds. They lasted a little longer that time.

"Queenie was next. Her first encounter was around Valentine's Day. This time it was Harris by himself. He was in a black car. Her pimp, Tyrone Washington, was watching the encounter from the front seat of his 1966, lime green, deuce-and-a-quarter (Buick Electra 225), which was parked across the street. Queenie and Harris agreed to a standard lay for $20, two emissions within 30 minutes, nothing extra. She knew Tyrone was clocking the time because he was greedy and didn't want any of his girls giving away anything for free, not even five extra minutes.

"She got in Harris's car and led him to a flophouse at East Main and 4th. They got out and she took him up to the 2nd floor to one of the rooms Tyrone rents for business. He's got four. She unlocked the door and stepped inside.

"Queenie stripped and Harris paid her. They got down to business, and then he started choking and slapping her. She started to resist and he hit her so hard, she blacked out. When she came to, she was lying on her stomach with a pillowcase over her head. Someone was holding her arms down while another man anally assaulted her. When she started to resist, the man holding her down slugged her in the face and told her to shut up if she wanted to live. That's when she became 100% compliant. The men took turns having sex with her both ways.

"At some point, they finished and one man used duct tape to bind her wrists and ankles. She recognized Harris's voice when he said, "Stay here for ten minutes before you leave or I will come back and kill you. Understand, bitch?" She told him she did, and they left.

"Since this trick took nearly an hour, she kept waiting for Tyrone to come and rescue her, but she learned later, he was sitting in his car getting a knob job from another girl in his stable who goes by the name, Breath of Heaven. Her real name is Denise something-or-other.

"The important thing here is, we now know the second man was Goetz, but she never saw him, nor does she know how he got there. Obviously, he had been watching and waiting.

"The last time was on March 16th."

Gonzo watched my expression and said, "Thought that date would ring your bell. Time wise, it occurred before they shot at you. They were feeling a bit froggy, and you'll understand why.

"Goetz was driving a light-colored van when he approached Sapphire, who was standing at the curb at East Main and 3rd. She pulled up her top and flashed her tits, and she's got some huge, really nice ones. He asked her how much, and she said $25 bucks. He said that was a little high and offered her $20. She smiled, pulled up her short skirt, and started rubbing her pussy. Then she licked her fingers and said, 'Sweet. Tight, too. You'll love it.'

"He asked, How about that sweet ass?'

"She responded, 'I saves that for special friends, but I'll let you have some for $40 bucks, but you gotta warm up my pussy first.'

"He said, 'Done deal.' Then he gave her two twenties and

she hopped in. She led him around the corner to the very same building Queenie went to. They went up to the 2nd floor, to the room next to Queenie's. She reminded him that all he paid for was 30 minutes while she undressed. He replied, 'If it takes me more than 30 minutes to quench my thirst thoroughly, then you ain't a very good whore.'

"Then they got down to business. They did it once vaginally and twice anally. He'd only been there 15 minutes, and he was done. She started laughing, and then he walked over to the door and opened it. Harris came in, holding a large hunting knife. She screamed and Goetz beat the living daylights out of her.

"Other than weeping, she shut up. Harris undressed and savagely tore into her anally. She said he was hung like a donkey and she'd never done a guy anally with a Johnson as big as his. He did her once each way, then Goetz did her again vaginally. She'd been engaged well over 30 minutes and she was desperately waiting for Tyrone to come rescue her.

"Tyrone didn't even knock. He just barged in the door holding his nickel-plated Smith & Wesson Model 10, .38 caliber revolver. He had a big smile on his face, and pointing to Goetz with his gun, he said, 'You a dead man, honky.'

"What he didn't realize was that Harris had been standing behind the door with that big hunting knife. Harris slipped up behind him, still in his nudies, and slit Tyrone's throat ear to ear. Tyrone fell to the floor, shuddered once, and bled out. Goetz jerked Sapphire out of the bed and mopped her face and body in Tyrone's blood. He said, 'Lick it up, or you're next.' She lapped up blood until the worst of it was gone.

"Both men washed up and got dressed. Harris said, 'We're

leaving now. If you so much as utter a sound or come out of this room before 3 o'clock, so help me God, I will find you and slice your throat just like his. Do you understand?'

"She nodded her head yes. They left, but she didn't leave until almost daylight.

"The maid found Tyrone's body about 9 o'clock that morning. She notified us. Until we started flashing both Harris's and Goetz's mugshots around, Tyrone Washington's murderer was an unknown male assailant. Thanks to you, when we catch him now, he's looking at the death penalty."

I replied, "Harris isn't going to surrender. He's going down in a blaze of bad man glory. The only way you catch him alive, is if you catch him in his sleep.

"You know, it's interesting that they were driving the van, because when they shot at me, they were in that black Ford."

"True, but consider this. They had ample time to go back to their digs, clean up, eat, and ambush you. They may have been expecting more drama - say a high speed chase, and wanted more horsepower and better handling. Besides, a black car is nearly invisible."

"You got that right. Did any of these girls have any information which might lead us to their pad?"

"Nope. That's the saddest part of all these stories. I wanted you to hear this so you wouldn't have any compunction if it becomes necessary for you to pop a cap on Harris. I know I won't if I happen to see him first."

"You're a good friend, Gonzo. If I pick up any leads, I'll let you and Beau know first. Thanks for everything."

"Ditto. Bye."

"Goodbye."

What do you do after you hear stories like these? I went back home and let the security force out. I smoked a cigar and nursed on some Old Dr. Crow neat. Those stories really haunted me. I was glad, thankful, that I never worked Vice. I didn't know how Gonzo did it. Just like medical examiners, I suppose. Somebody's gotta do it.

    I finally had enough elixir to go to sleep. I thought I was going to Vice to get a lead. Instead I got enough material for several nightmares. I fell asleep, wondering what happens next.

-16-
Marking Time

Two weeks passed without fanfare, except for the Kentucky Derby. It was the 99th Run for the Roses. Roscoe had a friend who managed to snag two extra seats in the bleachers up in the nosebleed section for 45 bucks each, so we went. We saw Secretariat win in a record-setting time of 1:59.4 minutes, 2-1/2 lengths ahead of the second-place horse, Sham. We didn't make any money to speak of on that race, but we bet on all the other races too, yours truly betting $2 to win on each race, and Roscoe ponying up $10 on each race, including some for win-place-show. He lost $42, and I came out $19 ahead. Roscoe's losses didn't break the bank considering how much he wagered, and I made lunch money for the next couple of weeks. We had a fabulous time.

The Derby reminded me of how thankful I was to be retired from the police force. Derby Week means 12 or 14 days straight, working untold hours due to all the festivities, to include the Pegasus Parade, the sternwheeler race between Cincinnati's Delta Queen and the Belle of Louisville (we usually lost), the Kentucky Colonels banquet and picnic, and countless other activities which were set up for the tens of thousands of tourists looking for Southern hospitality and a good time.

The pickpockets, ladies of the night, muggers, and car thieves always show up in record numbers, just like they do for major events in other big cities - events such as the Super

Bowl, World Series, Beatles, or Elvis Presley concerts. The Jefferson County Jail, designed to house about 500 inmates, is always bursting at the seams on peak event days with 700 to 1,000 lost souls cooling their heels. Fortunately, most are only charged with misdemeanors. Justice and law and order, meaning the police, never sleep. The overtime was great, but all the cops were relieved when the festivities were over and the drunks found their ways home, preferably without killing themselves or anyone else.

For a few local girls, there was one enormous benefit to Derby Day. Churchill Downs hired pretty girls, ages 16 to 22, to run bets for the high rollers who didn't want to leave their seats in the intervals between races, to stand in line and place them at the betting windows, which for high rollers were not all that far away. Churchill Downs didn't actually hire the girls, as in giving them a wage. Oh no! The girls made their money from tips. Betting is a cash only business, so no records were maintained, and whatever the girls made went straight into their pocketbooks. The IRS didn't get their cut. Too bad.

Each girl dressed in a short skirt, dressy blouse, and sneakers. Each was assigned a specific section with maybe 30 or 40 guests. The girls got better assignments with seniority, meaning they ran bets for guests in the pricier sections. In 1948, when Arabella was 16, she made over $200 in tips on that one day! The last year she did it, at age 21, she made $650! That was twice what I earned in a week! It was a godsend, and helped pay her way through nursing school.

Time passed without anyone in law enforcement laying eyes on, or getting a tip on the whereabouts of Wilbur A. Harris. It was frustrating. It seemed like everyone who wasn't a target forgot and moved on. C'est la vie. In the meantime, I slept with one eye open, not even going to the bathroom without my revolver because I knew he was still out there. Even KSP quit providing updates to Jake, probably because they didn't know where to start - just like me.

I was off on Saturday, May 26th. I needed some new jeans, and WalMart was having a sale on Wranglers. I drove to the one on Taylor Boulevard in my old Studebaker. I had returned the Valiant after the 30-day lease expired because it didn't deceive anyone except for myself. Certainly not my enemies. Checking for a tail was now engrained in me, but I didn't see any suspicious vehicles this day.

The store was packed and prices were great, so I picked up two pairs when one would have been sufficient. Ah! The thrill of saving money by spending money! I got in line to consummate my purchase. All the lines were interminably long with everyone saving so much money, so I had a considerable wait. Finally, there was only one customer ahead of me. I just happened to glance to my right and scared the bejesus out of myself. Wilbur Harris was standing right there, 20 feet away, raising his revolver to shoot me inside a store jam-packed with customers looking for a good deal! Besides nursing a vendetta, he had brass balls.

I ducked down behind the row of shelving filled to capacity with candy and other impulse-buying items. I unlimbered my own revolver, just as he cut loose with two missiles of destruction launched to hasten my demise. His first shot slew the cash register in my checkout lane deader than a doornail. I have no idea where the other projectile completed its dastardly journey. All I know is it missed. I snapped a hasty shot in return, but it whizzed two inches to the right of Wilbur's gargoyle melon, knocking a chip out of the concrete wall.

We both had missed our marks, but nevertheless, the gunfire frightened customers and clerks alike, all of whom were scrambling and knocking each other down to get out of harm's way via the nearest set of automatic glass doors.

Harris used the panicked public for cover as he fled outside. I was several seconds behind him due to the crush of humanity clamoring to get to safety, which reflected a far different mindset than my own. I had blood in my eyes. My mission was to remove Harris from the gene pool once and for all.

I saw him sprint to a white Ford pickup truck, maybe a 1968 model. He shot at me once more before he climbed in, but it was just to get me to back off. It wasn't an aimed shot. It posed a greater threat to the cars parked nearby than it did to me.

I emptied my revolver into his truck as he was squealing out, turning the driver's window into little shards of glass, not to mention perforating the door several times. He escaped in spite of my best efforts, nearly running over several spooked customers, and smashing into a red Volkswagen which got in his way. Disgusted, I reloaded, reholstered, and returned to the store.

An assistant manager named Jerry Perkins was ushering the few remaining customers outside the building. You know the ones - the elderly, the wheelchair-bound, those ambulating with a cane, and mothers herding three or four small children. The tough guys and able-bodied folks had long since abandoned ship. I reckon all the heroes stayed home that day.

I showed Mr. Perkins my retired police identification card and badge, and asked if anyone had called the police. By then, nearly all the customers were outside. He said they had, and the police were on the way. Then I went over and picked my jeans up off the floor and dusted them off. I asked if he could ring me up while we waited. He was as nervous as a man standing before a firing squad, but he acquiesced and rang me up. As soon as we completed the sale, three marked units rolled up, and four patrolmen rushed in, guns at the ready.

I walked up to the first patrolman, named Conrad Ebbetts, and displayed my credentials. I told him I was one of the shooters, and that Wilbur A. Harris, an escapee from Eddyville, was the other. I said Harris fled in a late model, white Ford F-100, license plate unknown, which I had peppered with shots, to include shooting out the driver's window. I said Harris had made three previous attempts on my life, and that I was working with Detective Lieutenant Beau Ames. He told another patrolman named McGillicuddy to put out a BOLO. Then he used the manager's phone to call Homicide, requesting that Lieutenant Ames be notified.

Then we waited.

While we did, Patrolman Ebbetts asked me what type of gun I carried. I responded that it was a standard .38 caliber Colt Police Positive.

He asked, "You mean the old .38 before they came out with the .38 Special?"

"That's the one. Bought it in 1925, the day I joined the police force. It's served me well for 48 years now."

"No disrespect, Sarge, but you need to upgrade to a .38 Special or a .357 Magnum."

"No disrespect taken. My boss, Roscoe Walton, retired LPD lieutenant, has been telling me that for years. I know the old, standard .38 ammo is getting hard to find, not to mention pricey, but I've got plenty stored up. I'm 69 years old, and I just don't feel like making a change. Besides, you have no idea how many villains I've shot or killed with this gun."

"How many would that be?"

"More'n a half dozen. Tell you the truth, I've lost track."

"Dern! That's more'n me, and I got 16 years on. Things must've been real hairy back in the day."

"Probably so, but we didn't see it. We thought it was just normal."

"Why's this guy Harris after you?"

"I arrested him and his partner ten years ago for raping a woman, after I shot him and his partner. They were taking turns brutalizing her. They got life. It was supposed to be without parole. They broke out of the joint on Christmas, and they've been after me ever since. This is the fourth time since then that they've shot at me. Now it's just Harris. I killed his partner, Louis Goetz, a month or so ago when they tried to ambush me at my home.

"You know. I was told LPD put this out with copies of their mugshots after that."

"Now that you mention it, they did. I forgot about it until just now. You know how it is. Each day at work presents its own challenges. It's not indifference. We just get busy."

"Right you are."

That's when Homicide and CSI made their appearances,

Detectives Alvin Winters and Ralph Bradshaw among them. Ralph asked, "Chet, you again? What the Hell?"

"Ralph, when you all gonna get around to corralling Wilbur Harris? I gotta do this all by my lonesome?"

"Well, you wouldn't have to go through it again if you was a better shot. I heard it was 0 for 6 today. That true?"

"It is. Maybe 'the old gray mare ain't what she used to be.' You know. Decrepitude on my part."

"Get outta here! I'm just busting your chops. If we knew where this oxygen thief lays his head, we'd take care of him for you."

"I know. Me too. No leads on his whereabouts yet?"

"This guy is a ghost. We know he's got to be robbing and stealing to make a living, but we haven't tied him to anything. I know Vice is hot after him, but either he jacks off to get his jollies, or he's found a squeeze that likes it rough. Now it looks like he's jacked himself another ride he has to ditch. Auto Theft needs to be looking for a report of a car stolen either today or tomorrow. That'll likely be him. Maybe it'll generate a lead."

"I hope so. You all want me to meet you downtown?"

"Yeah, if you don't mind. It won't take long. No dead bodies. Not much here for us or CSI to do. What say our office about 1:30?"

"You got it."

I had an hour-and-a-half, so I drove home (without a tail) and let the security force out while I made myself a couple of fried bologna sandwiches for lunch. I even had time to clean my gun and replenish my ammo pouch with fresh rounds. I counted my stash. I had 13-1/2 boxes of these standard .38s.

That should last me 'before I shuffle off this mortal coil' (William Shakespeare, *Hamlet*, Act III, Scene I).

I checked in with Jake before I went to Homicide. He asked if I wanted him to come down. I said no. Then I asked if he had any new developments. He said, "You and I wish. You're not the only one sitting on pins and needles. Beatrice is too, and therefore so are the Mrs. and I. Keep your powder dry and your fingers crossed. I'll be in touch."

I was in and out of LPD Headquarters within an hour.

I returned home and sat on my hands some more. I was getting really good at it. I wished Harris would call me up and say, 'Bring a gun at 12 noon and meet me at Louisville's Butcher Town corral, and come alone.' It also reminded me of what Mississippi comedian Jerry Clower said about a coon hunting misadventure. One night the dogs treed a coon up a tall tree and they couldn't get it down. One of the hunters climbed up to knock it out of the tree so the dogs could kill it. The coon was big and full of fight, and determined not to go. It started to maul the hunter, who yelled down to his friends, 'Shoot up here amongst us! One of us got to have some relief!'

That was the dilemma Harris and I found ourselves in. Harris wanted me dead in the worst way and the feeling was mutual. My Christianity was slipping bad. I wasn't planning to turn my cheek, or my back on that degenerate viper.

The days passed slowly with no developments regarding Harris - at least none that I knew about. I did my job at the fairgrounds, bought groceries, went home, played with the security force, slept when I could actually fall asleep, read a couple of non-fiction books regarding various campaigns during World War II, watched TV, went back to work, and repeated the cycle over and over again.

Wednesday eve, on June 13th, I up and called Arabella. She usually called me a couple of times a month so I didn't have to pay the long distance charges. Lucky me. She was home, and she answered the phone.

"Lee residence. Arabella speaking."

"Hey Girly, it's your papa. How you all doing?"

"Hi, Papa. It's so good to hear your voice. We're all doing fine. Did you know school's out? Fiona is already bored to tears. She's signed up for a book study on Wednesdays at the library. They read a classic novel over a two or three week period and discuss it during their meetings. Then they move onto another one.

"Barclay's playing baseball. He's on the Red Raiders. They have their first game tomorrow against the Green Devils.

"Randy and I still try to keep all our patients healthy. That's about it. What about you?"

"Oh, it's pretty much the standard routine. Been putting in a lot of hours. What else is an old codger like me supposed to do?

"Listen, I was wondering if you all would mind if I came down to visit for a few days. I haven't told Roscoe I'd like to take off yet. He won't mind, but I wanted to run it by you all first."

"Well, of course it is. We don't have any big plans. When would you like to come? You know Barclay's 9th birthday is coming up next week on Thursday. We could have a party."

"That sounds great. What if I drove up Saturday the 16th and returned home on Sunday the 24th? That be too long to put up with the likes of me?"

"Of course not. What about Dink and Bixby?"

"You know Bixby doesn't like to travel. He's set in his ways. I'll ask Herb and Amy next door to take care of him. He already spends a lot of time over there anyway. I think Amy sneaks him a few treats, but I'll bring Dink with. That be okay?"

"Perfect. See you sometime Saturday. Bring something to wear to church."

"Will do. See you Saturday."

Thursday morning I told Roscoe I'd like to take a week off to go visit Arabella and the grandkids in Richmond. He said tell me the days you want, so I did.

I went home, cleaned up, and did some shopping to get ready. I hadn't bought any clothes (besides the jeans) for four or five years, so I needed to do that. Then I needed to get a birthday present for both Barclay and Fiona. I knew what I wanted to get Barclay. I decided to get Fiona a necklace with her birthstone. Her birthday was in August, and I figured I probably wouldn't be there, so I decided to bring it with just in case. Arabella could stash it away until then.

Gifts first.

I went to Sumner's Hardware. Initially I had planned to get Barclay a .22 caliber, single-shot rifle, but Biff, the owner, suggested a 20-gauge, single-shot shotgun since Barclay would just be turning 9. It was a better gun for a young beginner, because shot from a shotgun only travels about 50 yards. A .22 long rifle bullet can travel a mile. Besides, he'd have fewer misses with a shotgun while he was learning to hunt.

Biff sold me on a Harrington & Richardson (H&R), which

only cost $39. I bought a cleaning kit for $4, a felt gun sleeve to store it in for $3, and two boxes (25 shells each) of Western brand number 6 shot, which is universally used for rabbits, squirrels, and pesky varmints. They were $1.50 each. Came to about $50, but who knew how long I would live? I might not see another of Barclay's birthdays. I wanted to give him his first gun.

I went to Ben Snyder's Department Store next. The clerk showed me a chart which said peridot was the birthstone for August. I bought a solitary peridot stone in a gold setting and a gold necklace for $55. They even gift wrapped it for me.

I decided to go clothes shopping for myself while I was there. I bought two pairs of khaki, pleated and cuffed cotton trousers, and five short-sleeve dress shirts - one pale yellow, one baby blue, one pink, and two white. I also got five diagonally stripped ties to go with. Ties were substantially wider than the last time I bought one, which was around 1959 or 60. Then I bought a forest green sport coat with gold-colored buttons, a pair of brown Florsheim wingtip shoes with soft soles, and a brown leather belt. While I was spending money faster than Congress, I decided to purchase a new Panama hat, a half-dozen pairs of white socks, and two three-packs each of boxer shorts and sleeveless undershirts. I went whole hog buying clothes for myself just like I was a woman, something I had never done before. If I owned a garment and it was not part of a uniform, it had been purchased by either Chloe or Arabella.

House gifts for the host and hostess and birthday cards were last. I bought Randy a fifth of Old Fitzgerald bourbon, and Arabella three bottles of Mondavi cabernet sauvignon. I got myself another fifth of Old Dr. Crow. I figured that was enough booze to get us through a week. Then I bought birthday cards at the pharmacy.

Finally, I stopped by the White Castle on my way home for a late lunch consisting of a half-dozen sliders and a 7-Up. They hit the spot.

Then it was security force time out back in one my Adirondack lawn chairs under the maple tree, coupled with a cigar and Old Dr. Crow. It was too late to go to sleep and have much impact before returning to work, but I tried anyway. It didn't help. It had been a full day and then some.

Thursday night was my last shift before going on vacation if you wanted to call it that. It was quiet, peaceful, somewhat boring, and uneventful - in other words, the perfect shift for someone who was my age. I stayed up when I got home Friday morning, cutting and trimming the grass, washing and cleaning the Studebaker inside and out, playing with the security force, grilling myself an early supper pork chop to go with my green beans, corn on the cob, cranberry sauce, buttered bread, and store-bought chocolate pudding for dessert.

I retrieved my old suitcase from the cellar. I purchased it just before Chloe and I went on our honeymoon in New Orleans, back in 1928. It probably looked a little dated. Who cares? Not I! It was medium sized, with an amber and brown tweed weave pattern, brown leather bolsters, and a brown leather handle. It looked really good, no scuffs, because it hadn't had much use. It did have a faint aroma of mothballs. I scrubbed it clean, inside and out, before packing all my new garments I wasn't planning to wear tomorrow.

The idea was for me to look spiffy every single day I was gone. Demonstrate to Arabella that I was doing just fine. She had suggested once that I sell out and move to Richmond. I suggested to her that she and her family move back home to Louisville. It was a Mexican stand-off, so we both shelved our suggestions. Hell! I'd walked the streets of Louisville for more years and many more miles than a vagabond twice my age! I was born here, and since the Japs and the villains had missed every opportunity they had to kill me, I planned to die right here and be buried next to Chloe.

That got me to thinking. I was done packing and it was still light, so I put the security force inside and drove over to Cave Hill Cemetery to spend some quiet time with Chloe. While I was there, I thought, what if Wilbur Harris followed me here and we had it out in the middle of all these tombstones? If he got me, I was already where I needed to be. If I got him, I'd make darn sure he was buried where he belonged - the Eddyville Prison Cemetery. I went home about dusk. The security force and I went back outside while I sipped on some Old Dr. Crow and smoked another fine Punch cigar. Then it was a well-deserved bedtime for all.

-17-
A Trip To Richmond

Saturday, June 16th, 1973. It was 62 degrees with clear blue skies, going up to 85.

I was in no hurry. The trip to Richmond was only a 100 miles or so. I decided to take the backroads instead of the Interstates. Make it more of a challenge for anyone who might be tailing me, especially since I was back in my 1950 Studebaker. Besides being an antique, it was dark blue over University of Kentucky blue. It stands out in a crowd, especially in Kentucky. I tell folks, "Don't let the color trick ya. I'm a Louisville Cardinals fan through and through."

After breakfast, I put on a pair of my new khakis with the yellow shirt and matching tie, plus the sport coat and new lid. I checked myself in the mirror. Amazing! I looked a whole lot better than a Fuller Brush salesman, even if I do say so myself! I put my suitcase, shotgun, and Dink's stuff in the trunk. Ditto for the gifts. I locked up and walked over to Herb and Amy's to let them know I was leaving. They already had my house key going back before World War II. (The locks still require a skeleton key.) I gave Bixby a head rub and received a small lick in return.

Then Dink and I piled in the Studebaker. I cracked the driver's window and opened both vent windows. I lit a cigar, and made my way over to Frankfort Avenue (US 60), also referred to as Shelbyville Road the farther east you go. We continued eastbound towards Frankfort, the commonwealth capital, roughly 60 miles from Louisville.

We took our old sweet time, stopping at a Sunoco filling station/cafe, so I could doublecheck for a tail while I topped off. I went inside and got a small cup of coffee to go. Didn't see any suspicious characters, so we moved on. The day was getting warmer, so I rolled all four windows down about three more inches. We drove south to Versailles, where I gave up the four-lane US 60 for the two-lane KY 169, which would take us into Richmond. Then I turned onto Tate's Creek Avenue and thence into the driveway of the Dr. & Mrs. Randall A. Lee family abode.

They called it a house. It wasn't. I live in a house. Houses are modest. This was a mansion, built in the 1880s by one of Confederate General Robert E. Lee's first cousins, a physician by trade, and more importantly, Randy's paternal grandfather. It was a brick, three-story, Greek Revivalist dwelling on three manicured, hardwood-filled acres. I felt certain my 1950 Studebaker, although nearly as pristine as the day I purchased her, probably should be parked in one of the five bays in the garage out back, and not in front of the house. What would the neighbors think?

Just then the entire family, including Basil, the brown bulldog named for Colonel Basil Duke, CSA, who was Confederate General John Hunt Morgan's brother-in-law, and successor in command of the 2nd Kentucky Cavalry, CSA, after his death. Basil the dog, came running out to meet us. Randy took my suitcase out of my hands to carry it into the 'house' while the others chattered over each other to greet me gushingly. Meanwhile, Dink and Basil introduced themselves in proper canine fashion by sniffing each other's butthole. Now their identities were forevermore logged into each other's mental Rolodex, never to be forgotten.

In deference to my advanced age, Dink and I were given the first floor visitor's suite. I'd stayed there before. Think of the Lincoln Room in the White House. It was that swanky.

It's quite nice, and very humbling actually, to be related - even if it is just by marriage - to southern royalty. I didn't fight it. I tried to blend in as best I could. After all, I had served in the Army too, just like Basil (Duke) and all the other Lees, even if it was the Yankee Army in World War II, in fact, the very same Army Randy had served with in Korea.

As the song *Dixie* attests, "Old times there are not forgotten. Look away! Look away! Look away! Dixie Land." Old times had been safely tucked away (in the form of Confederate artifacts and keepsakes) in a cedar chest upstairs on the second floor library, only to be aired on special occasions by southern gents sipping on bourbon and smoking aromatic cigars.

Arabella noted approvingly that I had 'dressed for success', and I continued to do so each day I was there. They all treated me like I was made of spun gold. Dink and I both had a hard time trying to live up to it. We didn't want to disappoint.

Saturday evening was pork barbeque and corn-on-the-cob with sweet potato pie and sweet iced tea out on the veranda, followed by a rousing couple of games of croquet on the back lawn. Afterwards, Randy and I sipped our bourbon from fancy crystal glasses and smoked our handcrafted cigars out under the white oak trees. Arabella and the 'chirren' came too. She savored on some chilled California cab, and the kiddos had root beer floats. When it got dark, we watched the lightning bugs put on a silent aerial display. It evoked some especially fond memories from my backyard when I was a child, and then when Arnie and Arabella were youngsters. I was thankful it was dark so no one could see the tears in my eyes.

Sunday was late morning services in Saint Matthew's Episcopal Church, followed by an ice cream social in the basement, which had more of the ambience of a lobby in an old, classic grande dame hotel than a dank church basement. It would have been a great venue for cigars and bourbon while studying the gospel. Back at the 'house' the supper menu was baked orange roughy on a bed of brown rice with mushrooms, pine nuts, shallots and uncooked halved cherry tomatoes, a wedge salad with bleu cheese dressing, and lime sorbet for dessert. The kids and I played checkers and Old Maid while supper was being prepared.

Monday Randy and Arabella returned to work. Fiona went to the home of her very best friend, Emma Beal, to play. Normally with Fiona, that meant something trending towards the academic, such as word games or putting together a 1,000-piece puzzle. Barclay had baseball practice, so Dink and I went with him to watch. For supper Arabella fixed country ham, biscuits, lima beans, applesauce, and bread pudding for dessert.

Tuesday, the kids and I stayed home. I took them to the local hardware store, where we bought the supplies to make a birdhouse. The design we chose was for bluebirds. We had it put together and mounted on a post before the grownups returned from work. That night Arabella fixed fried chicken, green beans, and mashed potatoes with white gravy for supper. We had fresh strawberries with whipped cream for dessert. After supper we all played several games of Sorry. Everyone but yours truly won a game. After we finished, Fiona said, "Grandpa, you're snakebit." Thinking about current events, I thought, "If you only knew".

Wednesday, I went to a drugstore and bought twenty packages of small balloons. Fiona saw what was up, and decided to stay home and play hooky from her book review session at the library. We had an epic water balloon fight in the backyard. Suffice it to say, we had no winners - only soaked losers, but we had more fun than the law allows. We cleaned up our mess and changed clothes just in the nick of time.

Arabella came home early because Barclay had a ballgame. That night we ate hot dogs, baked beans, potato chips, and cherry jello for dessert. We all rode in Randy's new, 1973, white over blue Cadillac Sedan DeVille. Barclay's team, the Red Raiders, beat the Blue Demons 4 to 3. Randy played first base. He grounded out to first, hit a blooper over the second baseman's head for a single, and struck out swinging. We went to the Dairy Queen afterwards for soft serve ice cream cones to celebrate.

Thursday was the big day. It was Barclay's 9th birthday. We were going to have a family party. He was all spun up, like he'd been feasting on cotton candy for 24 hours. Arabella came home at lunchtime to get things ready. My job was to keep Barclay occupied while Fiona helped her mom prepare. We went out back and played pitch for about an hour, but it wasn't enough stimulus.

Then Barclay had a better idea. We went in the garage and retrieved the cane poles and tackle box. He showed me where they bought bait at a convenience store, so we got a cardboard carton of crickets. Then we drove to the creek and commenced to fish. I caught two bluegills and he caught three, which we threw back so they could get caught another time by some other boy. He had lots of fun, especially since he caught the most and the biggest fish.

When we returned, Randy was setting the charcoal in the grill so he could cook the hamburgers. We also had potato salad, a relish tray, potato chips, Fritos, sweet iced tea, and of course a chocolate birthday cake with chocolate chip ice cream. Then it was time for Barclay to read his cards and open his gifts.

Fiona got him three comic books - a Batman, Superman, and Dick Tracy. They were a big hit.

Mama got him an erector set - another big hit.

Papa got him a Louisville Slugger, Pete Rose autograph model baseball bat (youth size). It was yet another big hit.

You know what I got him - a single shot, 20-gauge shotgun. It was the biggest hit of all, though Arabella had some reservations. Randy, being a hunter, thought it was great. Fiona said, "If he can have a shotgun, I want a bow and a dozen arrows for my birthday!"

Randy replied, "We'll see what happens. It's only two months away," and that pacified her because she knew she'd get it.

Friday, Arabella took the day off to spend some special time with me. Randy decided to close the office at noon. He and I were scheduled to take Barclay shooting after lunch. By the time Randy departed for work, both kids were busy following their own pursuits, so Arabella and I had some time alone. This was the moment I had been waiting for all week.

I handed her Fiona's birthday present and card, asking her to hide them for me. She asked, "Won't you come over to help us celebrate?"

"I hope so, but in the event something comes up and I can't, you'll be able to give this to her for me. Just so you know, it's a peridot necklace. I learned it was her birthstone.

"There's something I wanted to tell you about. Tonight when you and Randy are alone you can tell him."

"Oh my God! You don't have cancer, do you?"

"No. It's nothing like that. Let's get a lemonade and go out on the verandah. Then I'll tell you." Arabella makes the world's best lemonade from freshly squeezed lemons, and I needed one to bolster my courage since it was way too early for bourbon.

We went out back, and I told her the unsanitized version of the events which had transpired since February 22nd. I could see the horror in her face as I laid it out. She didn't utter a single word as she listened, but tears were rolling down her cheeks in a steady stream. When I was done, I shut up and waited for her response.

Finally, she dried her eyes with a tissue and asked, "There's absolutely nothing you can do is there? Nobody knows where this despicable Wilbur Harris lives, do they?"

"No. I'm afraid not. All I can do is keep my eyes open and my guns within arm's reach. I was afraid he might find me over here, but so far, so good. Problem is, he's a car thief and I have no idea what he's driving now. Forewarned is forearmed, and that's the best I can do for right now.

"One other thing. I've been writing a journal about my family history. It's what I know about my folks and siblings, to include what has happened in my life. Actually, it's in a looseleaf binder. I've been writing it for you so you'll have a better understanding of your heritage. If Harris manages to get the upper hand on me, I want you to look for it and read it. If I get him first, that will just be another chapter in the journal. Either way, I want you to read it when I'm gone."

"Did you bring it with?"

"Yes. I've been adding to it."

"I want to read what you've got now."

"The whole thing's in my chicken scratch, Sweetie. It's not ready yet."

"Go get it. I'll read it while you all are out shooting. Then I'll give it back. Please, Papa. I need to read this."

"Okay."

I went back to the Lincoln room and pulled it out of my suitcase. Then I handed it to her and said, "This is for your eyes only until after I'm laid to rest."

"Understood."

She retreated to the master bedroom upstairs, and I went out on the veranda and lit up a Punch. I wasn't sure I had done the right thing. Some of the material was pretty raw, and might revile her against me. I'd never have to know that if she waited to read this until after my demise.

Randy returned from the office. Arabella made us BLT sandwiches for lunch. Then Randy, Barclay, and I were off to a cornfield, the property of which he leased to a farmer. Randy picked this site because the crows were picking the corn clean. The scarecrows didn't scare many crows and the farmer needed the help. Neither Randy nor I brought our shotguns so we could concentrate on teaching Barclay; however, I did bring my Kodak, and I took a half roll of photographs.

The first order of business was firearm safety. I won't belabor the point because I figure anyone who might read this already knows all about it. Randy went over the procedure to load, fire, and reload this particular gun. He explained that shotguns are pointed, usually with both eyes open, not aimed with the off eye closed like a rifle, because shot spreads and single bullets don't. You don't have to be so precise with a shotgun. He also walked off the distance the shot would travel, and explained that it spread like a cone with distance. Then he placed some tin cans about five yards apart on the ground and told Barclay to see if he could hit them. Randy continued his instruction each shot as Barclay missed, until he finally got the hang of it and started obliterating the cans.

A crow landed on the top of a stalk of corn about 20 yards from us. Randy took the shotgun and blew it to smithereens. This put everything into perspective for Barclay. We walked over and picked up what remained of the Corvus so Barclay could fully comprehend the destructiveness of a shotgun. Randy explained the necessity of knowing what was behind the target before pulling the trigger. You don't want to hit someone or something unintended because it was behind your target. Then he told Barclay crows and blackbirds are the farmer's bane when it comes to their cornfields, and that they are always in season and you don't have to have a hunting license to kill them. We walked back to where we were. Randy handed the shotgun back to Barclay and said, "If a crow is dumb enough to get within range, see if you can put him out of his misery."

We sat on our hunting stools waiting for the crows to return. They finally did, one or two at a time, cawing all the while, and Barclay had a dozen or more opportunities to repeat his papa's performance. He missed all but one. Feathers went everywhere, but the crow managed to fly away. Randy said, "You hit it, and it will probably die. It's not what we want. We want to make a clean kill, but sometimes it just works out this way."

They'd gone through one of the two boxes of shells I brought, so Randy called it a day. We policed up the empty hulls and tin cans. We left the carrion for the buzzards. When we returned to the 'house' Randy instructed Barclay on cleaning his weapon. Then they placed it in Randy's safe with all of his long guns for safekeeping. It was a gratifying papa-son-and-grandpa bonding day. I'll never forget it. I prayed that someday in the not too distant future we could do it again, only next time on a dove hunt.

Fiona was watching television when we returned. Arabella was still upstairs in her room. She came down while the nimrods were cleaning the shotgun. She handed me the journal and asked me to join her in the parlor.

We sat.

After a lengthy pause, she said, "Papa, I learned so much that I didn't know. You've lived a dangerous life from the point you joined the militia right after high school. You've been shot at by outlaws and killed quite a few, even before I was born. You never once mentioned it, at least to me.

"You never spoke of that battle in Alaska with all those crazed Japanese soldiers. I swear I don't know how you survived. You've always been such a kind and considerate man. I would have said gentle, but that you are not. Your actions in combat belie that. I don't know how you can experience all this death and mayhem and still be so nice to everyone.

"I've always loved you, but your journal has intensified it beyond all bounds. I know what you're facing. I know what you must do. Just promise me you will take all precautions. I don't want to lose you, nor does anyone in this household. Promise me."

"I promise."

She rushed over and hugged me with an intensity that she had never shown since I announced my decision to enlist in the Army. Then she changed course abruptly and asked, "How was the shooting session?"

"Better than I could have imagined. Randy is a marvel himself when it comes to instruction. Barclay is a natural shooter. Now come hunting season, it's doubtful if you see much of them."

"That's okay. A team of wild horses couldn't keep Randy away from hunting. Why should I expect anything different from our son? I better go get ready for supper."

"What are we having?"

"Oh. I forgot you didn't know. Fridays are pizza night. We're going to Pizza Hut. Then we come home and watch the 9 o'clock movie. Tonight it's a rerun of Clint Eastwood's, *The Good, the Bad, and the Ugly*. I make a big batch of popcorn and we pig out."

"Perfect. I can't wait."

Saturday we went to the matinee and saw *Paper Moon*, staring Ryan and Tatum O'Neal. Afterwards, we returned to the 'house' and Randy grilled steaks for supper. He and I smoked more cigars and the grownups consumed more adult beverages.

Sunday we went to church. For lunch, Arabella made tunafish salad sandwiches on hoagie buns, served with cottage cheese, a relish tray, and chess pie for desert. Then it was time for Dink and me to head back to Louisville. As William Shakespeare coined in *Romeo & Juliet*, 'Parting is such sweet sorrow.'

I didn't tell them I had to be back to work at midnight. I knew I wouldn't get much sleep beforehand. Everything I got to do, and all the love we shared was worth losing a few hours of slumber. I kept a watchful eye out for a tail, but today I was spared.

Bixby was thrilled to see us. He richly deserved beaucoup attention, so of course I sacrificed some more sleep to accommodate him. At least I could sip on some bourbon and light up one of my favorite cigars while doing so.

I went to bed about 5 o'clock and rose at 10:45. I had virtually no food in the house, so I stopped by the all night White Castle for some yummy sliders and to get my thermos filled with black coffee. I arrived at work two minutes before my shift was to begin. It was the usual slow night. I managed to stay awake with coffee and by reading Sunday's *Courier Journal*, to include working its crossword puzzle.

I clocked out at 8 o'clock. I spent 15 minutes catching up with Roscoe. Then I dragged my weary behind out to the parking lot. I had to make a stop at the grocery before I could go home. 'No rest for the weary and the wicked don't need none.'

-18-
Not Again!

As soon as I pulled out of the parking lot, I saw Harris way back behind me once again in the black Galaxie. He had another man with him. I feigned ignorance and continued putzing along on my merry way like nothing was amiss. My fatigue had vanished like it had never been there. The adrenaline was flowing like a cold mountain stream. The problem was, my shotgun was still in the trunk! How should I handle this? I needed a plan, quick!

I kissed off the grocery. I made a quick right and turned into the Audubon Park Country Club parking lot. It was nearly empty. Harris followed me in. I parked and scrambled out of my car and retrieved my shotgun. I knew it was still loaded.

Harris pulled up and stopped about 30 feet behind me. He and his lackey both exited the Galaxie at the same time. Both had handguns. Harris was concealed by his car on the far side from me, but the lackey only had the passenger car door for cover.

I wasted no time. As soon as the lackey cleared the door, I approached him indirectly by circling wide and blasted him center mass. He fell to the macadam like a 150-pound sack of potatoes and never stirred, while Harris took advantage of the driver's side of the car for cover. He snapped a shot at me and missed because just then I scurried over to the passenger side of his car and ducked down. We were only the width of his automobile from touching one other. He didn't taunt me and I replied in kind. I suppose losing his sidekick so soon took some of the starch out of him. He was probably trying to figure out a way to shoot me without exposing himself to return fire.

I checked the lackey to confirm he no longer posed a threat. He did not. I ejected my empty and loaded another shell from the sleeve of five shells on the rear stock of the gun. For either of us to get a shot, somebody would have to move away from the car. Then I had an idea.

I lay on the ground and shot both his legs just above the ankles with one blast from the shotgun. He screamed and fell down hard. Then I finished him off with all six rounds in my revolver, which I parked in his torso. I reloaded both guns and walked over to see if he were still alive. His glazed eyes staring at the sky told me everything I needed to know. I had this burning desire to unzip and piss on his face, but I remembered that 'discretion is the better part of valor'. My ordeal was finally over. A wave of intense relief washed over my body like a soft summer rain. I would live in fear no more.

I placed my shotgun and gun belt and revolver into the trunk of my car. Then I waited for someone to call the police. Someone finally did, but I don't know whom, because I never saw anyone. Right now the parking lot was my own personal domain like Adam in the Garden of Eden, only this time Adam slew the serpent.

It didn't take long. A marked patrol car with its blue oscillating roof light finally rolled up, but not too fast. It was from the 5th Class City of Audubon Park. Two patrolmen got out of the unit and walked over to me. One's name tag read

Wahl and the other's read Black. I held up my retired LPD credentials for them to see. At least they noticed I was unarmed, and didn't point their guns at me like I was a dragon to be slain.

Wahl took my credentials and asked, "You do this?"

"I did. The one on the driver's side is an escaped convict from Eddyville named Wilbur A. Harris. I don't know the other one. Never seen him before. This is the fifth time in three months Harris has tried to kill me. LPD is aware of it and has all the reports. You all use LPD to conduct your homicide investigations?"

"Yep, on the rare occasion we have one. This is our first in over two years. Where's your gun?"

"In my trunk. I didn't want to get shot by a friendly. Look, when you all call this in, would you ask for Detective Lieutenant Beau Ames in Homicide by name? He'll want to see this."

Wahl returned my credentials before calling it in. It didn't take Homicide, CSI, or the Jefferson County Coroner's Office long to respond. When they did, Beau was the first to come over and talk to me.

"Damn, Chet. I guess it's true that if a man wants something done right, he has to do it himself. You all right?"

"Beau, you have no idea how all right I am. This has been going on for more than three months. Now I can finally sleep."

"No doubt about it. Walk me through it."

So I did. He replied, "Chet, you're a crafty opponent. I gotta give you that. By all rights you should be a dead man several times over."

"Thank you. Right you are. You know the only ending to this vendetta was with either Harris or me pushing up daisies. Harris just wouldn't let it go."

"Don't I know it, but he knew his days were limited. He chose this life. All it would take is him getting pulled over for a traffic violation or something else just as benign. I don't think he cared if he died. He just wanted to kill you first. You want to meet me up at CID (Criminal Investigations Division) in 30 minutes?"

"How about an hour? I haven't had a bite to eat since last night."

"You got it."

I thanked Wahl and Black before making a beeline to Frisches for breakfast. Then I called Jake. He said he would meet me downtown. I knew I was not facing a hostile room full of investigators. I just wanted Jake to come so he could join me in the closure of this tragedy, which began for him and his family 11 years ago.

Everything was cordial in Homicide. Jake and Beau and I sat around in the coffee room while the detectives and their clerks scrambled to put together all the details of this morning's double homicide. The good news for them is that the case was a quick closer, even including the presentation to the Grand Jury for a No True Bill against me. Apparently no witnesses came forth to make a statement, so my affidavit was all they had.

It turned out the lackey's name was Bruce F. Tompkins, age 38, from Cadiz, Kentucky. Harris and Tompkins had been cellmates in Eddyville for a couple years while he was serving a 10-year beef for aggravated assault on his boss at work. He had a job as a field hand, and he got pissed off while they were putting up hay so he stabbed him with a pitchfork. He had two other felony convictions, plus a list of misdemeanor arrests as long as your arm. He was out on parole, sponging off his sister in her one-bedroom apartment.

Bernice Coons, née Tompkins, was a twice divorced waitress in Cadiz, employed at the Happy Face Saloon on Main Street. She was paid $2 an hour, plus tips. She needed another mouth to feed about as bad as she needed a pet crocodile.

Bernice said Bruce had received a letter from some guy named Wilbur in Louisville, who asked if he wanted a job in Louisville which would only last a week. Said it paid $500. She told him not to go because it sounded shady, earning that much money in just a week, but Bruce said he knew Wilbur and it would be all right. He took the Greyhound Bus to get here, which she paid for because Bruce didn't have two nickels to rub together.

Wasn't Wilbur the name of a talking horse on a TV show, or was the horse Mr. Ed and his owner named Wilbur? She couldn't remember which. What kind of name is Wilbur anyway? Who besides Bruce would be dumb enough to trust a man named Wilbur, for God's sake?

Bernice said, "I'm done with Bruce. He ain't got no money, no insurance, no will, no job, no friends, no wife nor kids that I know of, and no broke-ass sister who's gonna to pay for his funeral. He done brought all this grief on hisself by being a worthless, no good, irresponsible piece of shit. Pardon my French. He can burn in Hell for all I care. Don't bother calling me again about Bruce. Plant him in a potter's field in a cardboard casket in an unmarked grave. Ain't no one here in Cadiz coming to his funeral, but I know a few who would piss on his grave if they knew where it was. Goodbye, detective!"

When we were done, Jake and I went back to his office. He pulled out a bottle of bourbon from his cabinet and a pair of fancy leaded, whiskey sour glasses. It was a top shelf bottle of Old Fitzgerald. He popped the cork and we had a taste. Then a second. We didn't clink glasses or even speak for the longest time. I reckon we were both caught up in our own private thoughts.

Finally, Jake said, "Chester, for the third time now - first the arrests 11 years ago - then the justified killing of Louis Goetz - and now the justified killing of Wilbur Harris - my family and I owe you a debt of gratitude we can never fully repay.

"If you are free on Saturday, I would like you to join us at my house for a cookout. We need to hash all this out and put it behind us forever. I want you to meet my wife and spend a few moments with Beatrice now that's she's all grown up and married. Come about 4. You bring the cigars. I'll furnish the bourbon. Are we on?"

"We're on. Thanks, Jake. Let me get outta here while I can still ambulate without falling down. I need some sleep. Good day, Jake."

"Good day, Chester."

I had to stop by the grocery and pick up some victuals. Then I called the fairgrounds and told Roscoe what happened. He was both distressed and relieved. He told me to take the rest of the week off. I told him I just needed tonight. Then I called Arabella at work and told her.

She asked, "It's over now, right?"

"It's over."

She said she wanted me to come back for a few days to celebrate Arabella's birthday. I said I would. She was relieved, just like me, before I rang off.

I sat out back and watched the security force frolic. I was too tired to imbibe any Doctor Crow without falling asleep. I did smoke a cigar. It was good to be alive and home.

Epilogue
1984

It's been over ten years since I've written a word in my journal. By the way, I've read George Orwell's book, *1984*, and I'm happy that all the radical changes he wrote about have not taken place - at least yet. Since the demise of Wilbur Harris and Louis Goetz, the drama I once experienced has abated to a trickle. Now my drama is centered around the passing of family and dear friends. I've attended many funerals.

I'm in great health for an octogenarian, but that's not to say I don't suffer from all the indignities as any other geriatric. At least I still have all my mental faculties.

I go to the indoor pistol range at least once a month to maintain proficiency from 10 yards. (I finally had to break down and buy a case of ammo, which cost this old Scotsman way too much dinero.) Also, now that I don't have anything better to do, I've become a regular attendee at the monthly FOP (Fraternal of Police) meetings. I want to know from the inside out what's happening in the City. In addition, sometimes I ride with Herb to the VFW to rub elbows with the other vets.

Big brother Angus Junior died three years ago, but Angus III has filled his shoes as an engineer on the old L&N railroad. Sadly, it was bought out by the Seaboard Coast Line two years ago, but what can you do?

Sister Phoebe is 84 now. Her husband Hiram's been dead

for six years, but their son, Ernest, took over running the bakery.

Brother Claude's 83 and still kicking, living in a mariner's rest home in Honolulu. We actually correspond every other week or so. I'm very pleased we're back in frequent contact after all those years of silence. Some motion picture studio should make a movie of his lifetime experiences. It would be a bestseller.

Brother Teddy is 81. He and Abigail are retired and doing well. We get together ever so often to eat supper, reminisce, and sip on Old Doctor Crow.

My lifelong next door neighbors, Herb and Amy Allison are still with us. They're about ten years younger than I. We look after each other like old friends do. Herb spends his free time over at the VFW, where he's the commander.

Both Bixby and Dink have gone to their feline and canine heavenly rewards. They're buried in my back yard. I made tombstones for their graves out of cement.

Bixby passed the torch to another tabby cat named Robert E. Lee, although he goes by Robert E. Dink has been succeeded by another rat terrier named June Bug. She usually accompanies me in my beloved old blue Studebaker wherever I go. She's beginning to show some age, but she gets me where I want to go.

I stop by Cave Hill Cemetery a couple of times a month to pay my respects to Chloe, Papa, Mama, and Junior. Sometimes I take a camp stool and picnic lunch and break bread while I'm visiting with them. I've found they're very good listeners. Also, they never scold me.

Arabella and Randy are still hard at it in their medical practice.

Fiona's a senior in Danville at Centre College, a liberal arts school. She's majoring in Political Science. She plans to attend the University of Louisville Law School next year. Hot diggity dog! I can't wait.

Barclay's a sophomore at Eastern Kentucky University in Richmond, close to home. He got a scholarship to play baseball. He's majoring in Finance. I usually go visit them once a month, especially if Fiona plans to be there for the weekend.

That sums up my life. God's been very good to me. Someday He'll call me Home and I will be able to see Chloe, Arnie, Mama and Papa once again. Until then, I'll keep putting out the flag each day, and taking care of my two wards, June Bug and Robert E.

God Bless.

Author's Other Titles

01-Making Mountains Out Of Molehills

It was 1969. Barlow Adams, age 20, was a recently discharged veteran. He was driving late at night on a lonely stretch of highway in the Trans-Pecos region of Texas. He stopped to render assistance to a motorist with a flat tire. What he stepped into was a vicious attempted rape. He rescued the victim, which catapulted him into a deputy sheriffs job.

02-When Dreams Come ~ True Sort of

The year is 1970. Barlow Adams is a young deputy sheriff in a rural county in the Trans-Pecos region of Texas. He's a rookie still learning the ropes. Up until now, his experience has been limited to working in the jail and performing routine patrol work that is anything but routine when bad men decide to exert themselves in furtherance of their wicked ways.

03-A Lethal Odyssey of Cat and Mouse

The year is 1971. Deputy Sheriff Barlow Adams and his fiancé, Sarah Baker, have just married. They've embarked on a motor trip through Texas to New Orleans for their honeymoon. An outlaw motorcycle biker that Barlow arrested and his cellmate have escaped from prison. They have the honeymoon agenda, and they're on a vendetta to murder both Barlow and Sarah, who are unaware of their imminent danger. Deputy Sheriff Archie Willis has been tasked with locating them to ensure their safety. It's a race against time.

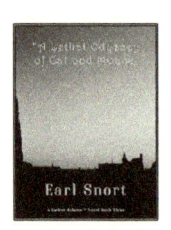

04-Evil Lurks In The Darkness, Even When Strong Men Stand Watch

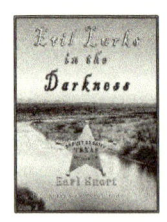

The year is 1972. Quayle County, located in the Trans-Pecos region of Texas, has seen an uptick of illegal alien smuggling from across the Rio Grande. The alien smugglers are determined and violent. The Border Patrol is overwhelmed with greater numbers of human trafficking cases in other areas, and therefore is unable to assist. So it is left up to the tiny Quayle County Sheriff's Office to protect the local citizenry and the illegal aliens by arresting the predatory alien smugglers.

05-Thicker Than Blood Murder, Hide & Go Seek Texas Style

The year is 1973. A four-man crew of stick-up artists has been on a rampage in South Texas along the Rio Grande corridor from El Paso to Laredo. One day they stick up the bank and liquor store in Mosby in Quayle County, killing one person and severely wounding another. Mosby is a small town in a large county, with only 3,000 souls and very little crime. Deputies Slick Oldman and Barlow Adams are tasked to locate and arrest the murderers.

06-Cleaning Out A Snake Pit, Before the Wheels Fall Off

It's 1974. Deputy Barlow Adams is on patrol in Quayle County, Texas, late at night. He initiates a traffic stop on a speeding truck. It screeches to a halt, and both occupants bail out, flourishing firearms. A gunfight ensues. One is killed and the other is wounded. A search of the truck reveals 60 kilograms of high-quality marijuana known as Oaxacan Highland Gold, or OHG for short. This leads to Deputy Slick Oldman and Barlow Adams being temporarily assigned to a DEA Task Force in El Paso. The stakes are high and the drug smugglers are deadly.

07-The Lawrence County Moonshine War - A Jack Rabbit Novel

This is a tale of a changeling shortly after these powers were bestowed upon him. Jack, who began life as a rabbit, fell asleep in arid West Texas shortly after wishing he had a home someplace else in a more temperate climate. When he awoke, he was a young man in a forest glen in such a place. He got exactly what he wished for! The problem was, he was wearing an Army uniform and he did not know his location. He didn't even know which century it was! Jack was suffering from a serious case of amnesia.

About the Author

Earl Snort is the nom de plumé of a retired law enforcement officer with 42 years' experience toting a badge and a gun. Before that he served in the armed forces. He and his wife have been married for 53 years. They reside in the South. They have one son, also a law enforcement officer, and two grandchildren.

This is the author's eighth foray into writing fiction. After a lifetime of writing non-fiction to document investigations of true crime, he decided to try his hand at make believe. He hopes you enjoy the yarn. Regarding the tombstone, it reads, "This site May 23, 1934 Clyde Barrow and Bonnie Parker were killed by enforcement officers." It's located near Arcadia in Bienville Parish, Louisiana.

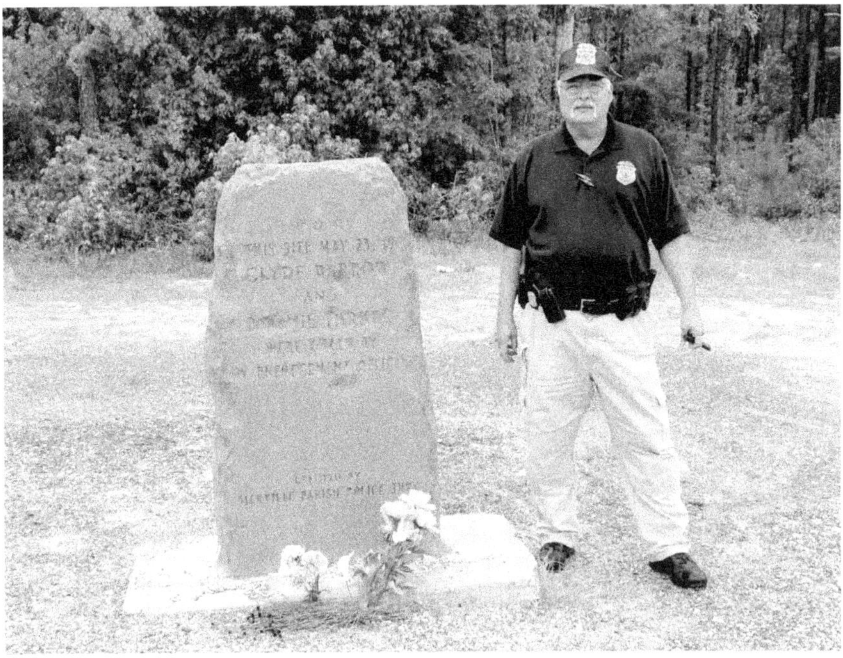